P9-DBQ-726

# Come Fall

Also by A. C. E. Bauer
*No Castles Here*

# Come Fall

A. C. E. Bauer

RANDOM HOUSE 🏠 NEW YORK

### ❧ To Emily and Abigail, of course ❧

This is a work of fiction. Names, characters, places, and incidents either are the product of the author's imagination or are used fictitiously. Any resemblance to actual persons, living or dead, events, or locales is entirely coincidental.

Text copyright © 2010 by A. C. E. Bauer
Jacket art copyright © 2010 by Tim Jessell

All rights reserved.
Published in the United States by Random House Children's Books,
a division of Random House, Inc., New York.

Random House and the colophon are registered trademarks of Random House, Inc.

Visit us on the Web!
www.randomhouse.com/kids

Educators and librarians, for a variety of teaching tools,
visit us at www.randomhouse.com/teachers

*Library of Congress Cataloging-in-Publication Data*
Bauer, A. C. E.
Come fall / A. C. E. Bauer.
p. cm.
Summary: Drawn together by a mentoring program and an unusual crow, middle
school misfits Salman, Lu, and Blos form a strong friendship, despite teasing by fellow
students and the maneuverings of fairies Oberon, Titania, and Puck.
ISBN 978-0-375-85825-3 (trade) — ISBN 978-0-375-95855-7 (lib. bdg.) —
ISBN 978-0-375-85826-0 (trade pbk.) — ISBN 978-0-375-85827-7 (e-book)
[1. Friendship—Fiction. 2. Foster home care—Fiction. 3. Junior high school—Fiction.
4. Schools—Fiction. 5. Fairies—Fiction. 6. Crows—Fiction.] I. Shakespeare, William,
1564–1616. Midsummer night's dream. II. Title.
PZ7.B3257Com 2010 [Fic]—dc22 2009032419

[Prin]ted in the United States of America
10 9 8 7 6 5 4 3 2 1
First Edition

Random House Children's Books supports
the First Amendment and celebrates the right to read.

# Contents

Come
Fall

But she, being mortal, of that boy did die,
And for her sake do I rear up her boy;
And for her sake I will not part with him.

TITANIA, QUEEN OF THE FAIRIES
William Shakespeare
*A Midsummer Night's Dream*
Act 2, scene 1, lines 135–137

# 1—Salman Page

**Rule number one: never be noticed**

Salman Page chose a table in the far corner of the Spring-falls Junior High cafeteria, next to a mural of brown and purple swirls—ugly, but he'd be harder to see against it. He kept his back to the wall and his head down, letting his shoulder-length hair hide most of his brown face. He wanted to be, to the casual observer, a kid intent on his meal of meat loaf and mashed potatoes. A few kids sat two tables away, not talking much. This part of the cafeteria was for losers. Salman thought that was just fine.

He glanced around once before he unscrewed the silver cap from his juice bottle, wiped it with his napkin, and slid it into his breast pocket. A skinny girl approached. She was midsized with short, light brown hair and a friendly face. Salman concentrated on his mashed pota-toes. The kids at the other table must know her.

"Hi," she said.

She was talking to Salman. He raised his head slowly. She smiled and pushed her glasses up her nose.

"Are you Salman Page?"

Who was this kid?

"Salman," he said, emphasizing the *L*. He wasn't some kind of fish.

"Sorry." She paused. "I'm Lu Zimmer, your desig-nated buddy."

She sat down and placed her lunch bag and a box of chocolate milk on the table.

Salman frowned. Because of a mix-up with his state files, his transfer here for seventh grade didn't happen until two days before school started. No one had assigned him a designated buddy. When Ms. R, his homeroom teacher, had asked him whether he got along with his d.b., he had no idea what she was talking about.

"Deebee?" he said.

"It's short for designated buddy," Ms. R said. "An eighth-grade mentor."

"Don't have one," he said.

Ms. R radiated disapproval.

"I'll make the arrangements."

Salman didn't need a designated buddy. He wished Ms. R had never asked him about it.

Lu Zimmer plowed ahead.

"I'm supposed to meet with you, walk you around the school, show you how things work. That kind of stuff."

"I've walked around already."

School had started a week and a half ago. What did she expect? Lu hesitated.

"Maybe we can talk about your teachers."

Salman was about to tell her that he didn't need to talk about his teachers when they were interrupted.

"Hey, Lu!"

A gangly white boy with wiry orange hair and a face full of pimples lurched over, carrying an oversized lunch bag. He was very tall.

"May I join you?" he said.

Before either Lu or Salman could answer, the boy sat down next to Lu and emptied the contents of his sack onto the table.

"I heard Ms. R made you a d.b.," the boy continued in his too-loud voice.

Lu reddened, and her smile strained.

"Salman Page," she said, "this is Blos Pease."

Blos turned to Lu.

"You are his d.b., right?"

"Yes, Blos," Lu said.

Her smile was fading. Blos focused on Salman.

"Did you know Lu and I had the same d.b. last year?"

Salman gave only the slightest shake of his head.

"It is true. We used to have lunch with her, all the time."

This last statement refocused Blos onto his own lunch. He removed the items from each of the four separate sandwich bags and lined them up in front of him.

Blos took a deep breath, hands hovering over the sandwich. He blinked at Salman and let his hands drop.

What now? Salman wondered.

Blos's lower lip covered his upper. He stared hard at Salman. His hands kept approaching his sandwich and then retreating. Salman almost looked forward to what was going to happen next.

"Where are you from?" Blos asked.

Salman hated that question. Adults who felt they needed to make conversation, teachers who thought ethnic backgrounds were important, even the occasional idiot social worker who should have known better at some point asked: "So, where are you from?" Salman had dark skin—darker than most African Americans—angular Caucasian features, and straight, glossy hair. "You have South Asian parentage," someone once told him. Over the years, whenever he could get to a library, he read books about India, Bangladesh, and Pakistan. Still, he had no idea where his parents came from. He was a foster child, had been since birth, with no known parents.

But Salman had met kids like Blos before. They stood out in every school he had been in. They liked things organized, in their place. Blos had asked the question for the same reason he had set up his lunch in a line. There was an order to things in this boy's world. He needed to find Salman's place in it to be able to move on.

"I'm from Bridgeport," Salman said.

"I have a cousin in Bridgeport," Blos said.

Salman almost felt a "Made in Bridgeport" label being stuck to his head as Blos filed Salman behind his cousin from Bridgeport in his mind. Salman grinned.

Blos now put all of his energy into eating his row of food. He stuffed the peanut butter sandwich into his mouth, followed by the carrots, followed by a sliced apple, followed by several cookies. He was moving so fast, Salman saw it all as a blur.

Lu gave a nervous laugh.

"You have cousins everywhere, Blos."

Lu was trying to smooth things over. She didn't have to. Salman didn't mind him. Everything about Blos was out in the open. He had asked a question that mattered to him, had received an answer that made sense, and now everything was okay. That was okay with Salman, too.

"I have to go," Blos said, food still in his mouth. "I have to finish an essay for Ms. R."

He swept the remains of his lunch—empty plastic bags and a few crumbs—into his sack and was gone.

Salman glanced at Lu, questioning. She shrugged.

"Blos doesn't have too many friends," she said.

Salman related to that. He ate the last bite of his meat loaf.

"I didn't know you were from Bridgeport," Lu said.

"I was born there."

Found there, he thought. Didn't stay. Why was this girl bothering him?

"I'm from Springfalls," Lu said. "Been here all my life."

She sounded wistful, as if she wanted to move. What did she know?

Salman stood. "Gotta go."

"Wait," Lu said. "We haven't talked about your teachers." She almost sounded panicked.

"I've got study hall in five minutes."

Lu glanced at the cafeteria clock. "Can we talk after school? We can meet at the bleachers."

She just didn't give up. He was about to refuse but worried that Ms. R might find out. And she'd ask him—very nicely, he was sure—if there was anything she could do to help. As if.

No point in getting himself noticed.

"Okay. Just for a few minutes."

As he retrieved his pack, his irritation grew. He didn't need a designated buddy. Just because Lu was in eighth grade didn't mean that she knew more than he did: she was probably a whole year younger than he was. This was his eleventh school in nine years. He had seen more teachers than she ever would.

8

And the name "designated buddy" was so stupid. Since when did people go about designating friends? He wasn't going to be in this town long enough to have any friendship stick, not with the foster home he was in.

He turned left to head down the corridor and saw Lu throw her lunch bag into the trash. It arced perfectly and landed, clear center. Swish. Not bad.

# 2–Puck

### In exchange for a pie tin

They bickered about the boy. Again. As if he were a bairn!

"Why do you concern yourself with this mortal?" King Oberon asked.

"Because I told his mother I would," Queen Titania replied.

"You promised me that you would leave him be!"

He was jealous, my king, jealous of any creature that my queen coveted. Jealous that her affections were not his to govern. And my queen . . . my queen knew he was jealous. She reveled in his jealousy.

It was my fault, of course. It was *always* my fault. My vanity. I had decided to wear the cursed bracelet in my queen's presence. Best if I had left it hidden.

"Puck, what have you there?" my queen asked.

"A golden circlet."

So finely wrought. It fit perfectly on my wrist. I had traded it from a friend, a crow, for a human's discarded pie tin. Crows love shine—and the tin shone so much more than the circlet.

"I know that circlet," the queen said. "Let me see it, Puck."

Her eyes narrowed. A frown creased her forehead.

"Where did you get this, Puck?"

Her fist closed over the slim band, no longer mine, I knew. My heart sank.

"I received it in fair exchange."

This angered the queen beyond measure.

"Miserable Puck! *What* could you exchange that would equal this gift?"

I did not expect her anger. I thought fast. I was bound by truth—I could not tell a falsehood to my queen or king.

"The crow received a pie tin."

That surprised her. Enough to distract her fury from me.

"Crow?"

"Yes, Your Majesty. I recognized the faery gold and offered the tin in trade."

This was truth, but an incomplete truth. I had offered the tin in trade first, then recognized the faery gold. But I had not lied to my queen.

"And where did the crow say he found the circlet?"

This I had an answer to.

"Nimuë's island."

Cursed is the name! I knew Nimuë was in the queen's disfavor. I knew my queen and king had argued about his fondness for the enchantress. How was I to know that the circlet had been a gift to my king from my queen? And that the only way it could have found its way to Nimuë's island was for King Oberon to have brought it there?

So the queen sought revenge. Oberon's jealousy. And I, poor Puck, *I* was sent to run her heartless errand of finding the one thing that angered the king beyond measure. The boy.

Pah! The boy was almost a man.

# 3—Lu-Ellen Zimmer

### A murder of crows

Just her luck, this year—Lu finally became a d.b., but her assigned student didn't want to have anything to do with her. She wondered whether Salman would be at the football field. Maybe, she thought, she'd be better off if he didn't show. The last thing she wanted was to deal with someone hostile.

Not that she blamed him, not entirely. Springfalls Junior High was, well, pretty white. There were a few African American students in each grade, a handful of Latinos, and a bunch of Asians, but no one was as dark as Salman. And he was so skinny, with a hungry look around his big, light brown eyes. His well-worn clothes dangled on his frame. And he seemed older than the other seventh-grade kids. He might almost have stubble on his chin.

Maybe that's why he seemed so self-possessed, as if he didn't need anyone or anything. He probably figured she was just another stupid, young white kid.

Lu really didn't know why Ms. R thought he needed a designated buddy. She had made it sound easy.

"Just do whatever your d.b. did with you last year."

Right. Lu's d.b. had been given a package of orientation materials over the summer, was told who Lu was at least a week before school started, and had even met with Lu on the day they received their class assignments so they could go over them together.

"He's new in town," Ms. R said. "You'll be a great help."

Lu couldn't say no. She had volunteered late last spring, well past the deadline. She had pleaded with Ms. R—being chosen as a d.b. was something of an honor, and Lu had really hoped to meet new people, now that Frances was gone. Ms. R told her then that Lu might not be assigned anyone—the other volunteers would be chosen first. Lu should have been happy that Ms. R found Salman.

But what was Lu going to tell this boy who was so reluctant to speak with her?

Turned out, Salman was waiting for her. She counted that as a small miracle. He had chosen a spot about a third of the way up the bleachers. Not at the top, where kids might think he was out to prove something; nor at the bottom, where they might think he was timid. He was trying to be inconspicuous. At least, that's what Lu figured.

He watched her as she climbed the steps. She smiled—just to let him know she was friendly. When she was close enough, she said hello in a quiet voice. She could be inconspicuous, too.

Salman nodded in response. She dropped her pack at her feet and placed her polished vinyl flute case beside her on the bench.

"I have a lesson in half an hour," she said, "so I can't stay for too long."

He'd appreciate that she didn't plan on wasting his time.

"Okay by me," he said.

An awkward pause followed. She needed to break this ice.

"Salman's a cool name. Is it short for Solomon?"

He shrugged and stared away from her, down the track, avoiding all eye contact. Just great. Best to plow ahead, she decided.

"So. Who are your teachers?"

He rattled off their names, one after another, in quick succession.

"Ms. Jones. Ms. Frankenfrantz. Mr. Ho. Ms. Carver. Mr. Loengredl. Ms. R."

Lu had had all but Mr. Loengredl last year and had Mr. Ho and Ms. R again this year.

 Simsbury Public Library
Children's Room

"Ms. R is really good. You're lucky to have her for Language Arts."

"She gives a lot of homework," Salman said.

"Yeah, but she's fair and funny, and she assigns really good books."

Salman shrugged again, staring at the football squad working out on the field.

Lu didn't give up.

"Now Mr. Ho, he can be tough. . . ."

Salman's gaze moved past the field, past the kids running track around the perimeter, to the fence of the neighboring baseball field. She wanted him to pay attention to what she was saying. She spoke faster.

"His labs are the worst. He wants them just so, and doesn't tell you how that is, and you waste hours doing reports over and over until he tells you they're okay. . . ."

But Salman wasn't listening. He had focused on a bunch of tall trees at the far end of the fence. No, she realized, he was focusing on a bunch of crows who flew over the trees and cawed to each other. A murder of crows.

She let her voice trail off. One of the crows, larger than the rest, broke from the flock and flew over the playing fields in their direction. Salman's eyes were riveted on the bird.

Lu gasped. It was headed straight for them!

It circled overhead, then swooped once, twice, and

for a split second, like magic, Lu was the crow, air whooshing through her wings. It landed next to her music case.

Lu's heart raced.

The crow tilted its head to look at her with one eye, then hopped sideways onto the case and pecked at the vinyl handle.

"He likes shiny things," Salman said.

His voice allowed her to breathe. She tried to speak, but words just weren't coming out.

Salman whistled. The crow cocked its head, hopped twice, and flew up to Salman's shoulder. Those claws looked sharp, but Salman didn't wince. He fished out a bottle cap from his shirt pocket.

The bird's head darted forward. It grabbed the bottle cap with its beak and flew off.

"Wow!" Lu said.

Salman grinned, showing off big white teeth.

"Did ya see that?" someone yelled from the field.

"He fed him. . . ." "Right on his shoulder. . . ." "Jumped to his whistle. . . ."

Kids began approaching the bleachers in groups. To Lu, they seemed curious. Admiring, even. But Salman's shoulders folded forward. His hand clutched his pack. He wanted to run. He was scared.

Okay. She'd defuse this. Lu caught his panicked eye and gave him a small smile, hoping he'd understand her signal to remain calm. Then she stood, pointed in the direction the crow had flown, and yelled, "Look! It went that way!"

The kids below turned and started running toward the baseball field.

"Did you see where it went? . . ." "Got anything to eat? . . ." "A *big* one. . . ."

It worked! The kids were concentrating on the crow, not Salman.

"Come on," she said.

Salman followed. They climbed down the bleachers, Lu setting the pace—not too slow, not too fast—and headed back into the building.

"Thanks," Salman said.

"No problem," Lu said.

They walked toward the practice rooms by the auditorium. That's when Lu noticed how tall Salman was—taller than most seventh-grade boys. But not the tallest. Boys came in all sizes in junior high. Blos had towered over them all, last year.

She stopped at the corridor where she needed to turn off. Salman stood and shuffled.

"How did you know?" he said.

Something tugged at her—she couldn't figure out what. She hadn't expected to see him so vulnerable.

"No one wants a label," she said.

Salman smiled, a bit of his hard polish returning. "Bird Boy."

"Something like that."

Salman softened once again.

"Thanks," he repeated.

That's when she sensed the *ping*. Something hit inside her and vibrated in a good way. She swallowed.

"Is the crow . . . your pet?"

"No. He's just a friend."

What a friend!

Salman placed a hand on one of his pack's straps, a signal he wanted to leave. But she could tell he was also hesitating.

"See ya soon," she said. "Okay?"

"Okay."

He had said it as if seeing each other again might be a nice thing. And she thought, as she watched him go, that being Salman's d.b. might be a nice thing, too.

# 4—Salman Page

**The most beautiful flowers on this green earth**

Salman had missed the school bus, so he walked the several miles to the Royals' trailer on the town line, skirting the woods around the trucking property that cut the Royals off from the rest of town. He spent the walk berating himself. He had let himself be noticed! Rule number one: never be noticed. And why did he tell Lu Zimmer about Bird? Rule number two: the less people knew about him, the better.

When Salman reached the dirt driveway, Tina Royal was standing on the trailer's stoop, her form filling the doorway. She wore her gardening pants: enormous overalls with blackened knees and a year of dirt on them.

"Late today," she said.

"Met my designated buddy," Salman said.

"Humph!"

Salman wasn't sure what she meant.

"We're harvesting tomatoes," she added, "before to-morrow's rains."

Salman nodded. If Tina said it would rain tomorrow, then it would rain.

"I'll just drop my pack," he said.

As Tina stepped down to let him through, he heard the *ka-chunk* of an industrial-sized stapler forcing inch-deep staples into wood. The sound came from the garden below the trailer. Ozzy Royal was building his fence.

"Tired of them deer eating Tina's produce," Ozzy had said.

He had begun the work two weeks ago, at a fever pitch, tirelessly digging holes for posts, sawing wood to proper lengths, propping up chicken wire and stapling it on. But after a day or so, he had slowed down. Now, with the fence three-quarters done, he behaved as if the project wasn't worth it. He hadn't put up a new post in a week, and two bales of the wire sat untouched by the side of the driveway. Tina had been after him to fill in the big gap left at the bottom of the garden.

"I'm waiting," Tina said.

Salman jolted himself back to the present.

"Coming."

He rushed into the trailer, threw his pack onto his

bed, and rushed out. His stomach growled. He wished he had snagged a snack—dinner was still hours away.

He grabbed one of the bushel baskets behind the trailer and ran past the chicken coop. The garden had been planted in a wide plot of black earth within a slow bend of the creek at the edge of the property.

The Royals grew vegetables. A huge, gigantic amount of vegetables. Salman didn't understand how anyone could plant so many, in such variety, with so much success.

"The most beautiful flowers on this green earth," Tina said.

As each vegetable ripened, Tina canned it—mason jars lined the innumerable shelves in the root cellar.

Salman knew the root cellar only too well. The day he arrived, he had refused to help in the garden.

"Now, honey," Tina had said, "it's where we get our food."

"The state gives you money for my food."

Ozzy's pasty white face turned beet red.

"Don't you go worrying about no money! Tina asked you to help out, and you're going to help out!"

The large man, the size of a linebacker, loomed over Salman and curled his hand into a fist. Salman shrunk back. Ozzy opened the trailer door and placed his power-ful hand on the back of the boy's neck. He marched Salman to the garden, gave him a bushel basket, and made him pick peas.

"Faster!" Ozzy yelled.

He stood over Salman the entire afternoon while Salman picked row after row. The late June sun beat down and Salman grew thirsty, but Ozzy didn't allow him a break. When the third basket was almost full, Tina showed up with two glasses of water.

"Drink up, hon. I'll bring more later."

That evening Ozzy locked him up in the root cellar.

"So you can see where your next meal is coming from."

Salman didn't see anything. There was no light. The root cellar had been dug out of the earth into a rise of land near the woods. Ozzy and Tina had placed beams to hold up the ceiling and a wood frame for the door, and had built shelves throughout. But the walls and floor were packed earth. There were no windows. Once the door was shut, no light peeked through. And it was cool.

Salman shivered in the dark in his shorts and T-shirt, huddled into a ball, terrified that bugs were crawling over him, that an animal might be snuffling in a corner. He didn't dare move: in the blackness, he was unable to see his hands or feet and he thought that if he stood up, he might knock over the glass jars, cut himself, and bleed to death.

He didn't sleep. He cried some. He had no idea how long he stayed in there.

When Tina opened the door in the morning, the light framing her bulk hurt his eyes.

"Best not get Ozzy angry," she said. "I've got a bath and breakfast ready for you."

Ozzy wasn't around when Tina took Salman to the trailer. She showed him his small room and bed. She had a threadbare towel ready for him, and some old clothes.

"Used to be Ozzy's. I've taken them in a bit."

The stitching scratched, but Salman didn't complain. Much later he learned from his social worker that Ozzy made the state pay for the clothes.

Over the summer, Salman worked the garden, the one thing about him that seemed to please Ozzy. He learned to weed and water, dig up potatoes, pick peppers, and cut lettuce. To his surprise, he began to enjoy the work. He had no idea what Tina had done to that soil, but each plant bore something remarkable—out of sun, water, and earth grew enormous squash, long cucumbers, succulent corn. Every week they ate something new and delicious. He no longer minded spending his time in the sun or rain or even with the bugs. And when Ozzy wasn't around, Tina was okay company.

Besides, it was far better than what came next: canning. That meant washing and chopping vegetables, standing over steaming pans and boiling pots, and handling scalding jars, always on hot days.

When Salman wasn't in the garden, he cooked, cleaned, raked, did whatever Tina and Ozzy told him. The only chore he wasn't asked to do around the property was to gather eggs. That was Tina's department. She always knew where to find them.

"Them chickens were the best investment we ever made," she said.

Salman was never forced to return to the root cellar, at least not as punishment. But Ozzy never let him forget the place, either.

"Remember where your food comes from," Ozzy said.

Salman began picking tomatoes. He filled the basket, gently placing the tomatoes one next to the other, in an array of reds, oranges, and yellows. The fruits were smooth and warm to the touch. He sniffed one, relishing its sweetness.

Ozzy stared at him from a newly planted fence post.

"Put the tomato in the basket," he said. "Don't waste time."

The rebuke cut like a whip. Salman flinched and threw the tomato into the basket. It broke when it landed.

"Caw!"

Bird flew onto a tree branch at the edge of the garden. He hopped once and tilted his head. For a second, Salman saw himself as Bird did—a tall, thin boy in worn hand-me-down clothes, crouched among fruit-laden bushes.

Salman smiled at the crow but kept working. Then from the corner of his eye he saw Ozzy lean over and pick up a pebble.

Salman called out, "He won't do any harm."

"Don't like crows near my garden," Ozzy said.

The large man threw the rock at the bird. He missed his mark. But Bird stretched his neck and flew off with another caw.

Anger welled. "Bird's my friend!" Salman wanted to yell. But he didn't. Ozzy didn't care. He only had feelings for Tina—and even then, Salman wasn't always sure.

Tina, who had been harvesting a few rows over, stood up at that moment, hands on her lower back. She was a large woman, even larger than Ozzy, and Salman saw her mass shift under the overalls as she straightened. She picked up her basket, now brimming with tomatoes, and walked over to Ozzy.

She said something Salman couldn't hear. Ozzy growled something back. Salman recognized the tone— irritation and anger, pulling at the man as if they were beasts on a leash. Ozzy was picking a fight.

Tina responded in kind, her voice sharp. Salman caught a few words.

". . . help . . . polite . . . quiet . . . extra cash . . ."

"He's underfoot!" Ozzy yelled.

They were arguing about Salman. He knew that. The cash Salman's fosterage brought in usually kept Ozzy pacified—that and the fact that Salman did most of Ozzy's work in the garden. But the man had been brooding lately. Salman wondered how many days he had left.

His previous placement had lasted a little over a

year—the longest since his first, when he had been given his name. But Mr. D had lost his job, and he and Ms. D had decided to move down to North Carolina, where she had family.

"Wish we could take you," she had said.

Salman didn't believe that she had meant it. No one wanted a teenage boy. Ozzy Royal certainly didn't. Tina was the one who had signed up with the state. She had told Salman once, "I always wanted a kid of my own." And she did try to be nice. But ever since Salman arrived, Ozzy had been complaining about him.

The man threw down the stapler and stomped away. Tina paused a moment before glancing at Salman.

"Finish up," she said. "I'll be in the kitchen."

Salman sighed in relief that Ozzy had left the garden, and in weariness at the afternoon ahead.

He reached out for the next tomato and stopped. It was a perfect sphere, no bigger than a Ping-Pong ball, hanging from a slender stem.

Salman plucked the tomato. With a quick glance over his shoulder, he popped it into his mouth. Tasted as sweet as it smelled, he thought.

He swallowed. Did Lu Zimmer like tomatoes?

He stood. Where did that thought come from?

# 5–Puck

### The loyalty of friendship

I spied, yes, as Queen Titania demanded. But I would spy as I chose!

"The crow?" she cried. "You receive news from the crow?"

I bowed low. 'Twas my role. To bow low.

"Yes, my queen."

"Crows aren't loyal to us."

To the truth, crows were indifferent to us. The queen disliked their dark plumage and cunning ways. But crows and faery were kindred, truly. I did not say this, of course. I saw no reason to increase her ire.

"He is a friend, milady."

"A friend? This crow?"

"He is indebted to me."

That, my queen understood. Debts.

"How?" she said.

"I was in search of feathers," I explained, "for the carnival, for my costume."

"Craftwork, Puck."

She disdained all handiwork, as it was reserved for those below her. But I found pleasure in craft, when wrought to good purpose. Again, this was not something to tell my queen.

"Indeed, Your Majesty. But I found the bird beset by an eagle."

"An eagle? Why would an eagle bother with a crow?"

"The murder had harassed her nest. The eagle sought revenge."

Revenge was something else my queen understood well. She nodded in approval. I chose my words carefully.

"I did not intend to interfere."

This caused a frown.

"But you did, Puck."

"My appearance startled the birds."

Now I had piqued her interest rather than her ire. Good.

"What did you do?"

"Naught, milady. Naught. I swear. I simply . . . appeared."

She laughed then, forgiving my trespass.

"Indeed, Puck. I am sure you did."

She paused and collected herself.

"You are overly fond of dark birds."

"But hear, milady. Out of gratitude, the crow offered me the loyalty of friendship."

"And you accepted?"

I nodded. Her smile was cold.

"Friendship has liabilities of its own, Puck."

I bowed again.

"Yes, milady, but in this case it was wise."

"Puck? Wise?"

I stood a touch straighter.

"In this it was, milady. For the boy is friendly to crows."

She shook her head, unbelieving. "At his birth, I gave him the gift of grace, not the ability to speak to other beasts."

"He does not speak the bird's language, milady. But they understand each other, nonetheless."

She seemed pensive at that. "That is a gift of its own."

"Indeed, milady. Perhaps it comes from his father."

She waved that away. "He was just a man. His mother, more like."

I had been curious of the provenance of this child, this thorn in Oberon's side.

"She understood birds?" I asked.

"She tended a garden for her mistress. The place was renowned for its flowers, which attracted all manner of birds and curious insects. I decided to visit it. It was entrancing, which may explain why I allowed my disguise to drop. She saw me and mistook me for a god. She treated me with garlands and sweets. I returned—the place was attractive and the woman faithful and compliant, even as her belly grew. In her way, she understood birds."

"As the boy does the crow."

She nodded. She was not pleased by the crow, but tolerant. I would need to tread carefully.

# 6—Blos Pease

### Nothing out of place

Blos Pease put his notebook, biology book, four-color pen, pencil, eraser, ruler, and graph paper on the table. He tore the first sheet of graph paper from the pad, then wedged it into the pad so that it was not obvious that it was loose. The pad went under the notebook. The textbook was on his left. His pen, pencil, eraser, and ruler were lined up above. Nothing was out of place. He had three minutes before the homeroom bell. Mr. Ho walked in.

"Good morning, Blos."

"Do we have a dissection today?" Blos asked.

Science lab with Mr. Ho came after homeroom.

Mr. Ho shook his head.

"Not today, Blos. We'll be using the microscopes."

Blos sighed in relief. Good. He hated dissections. They made him feel queasy inside. Anything that made him feel queasy inside was no fun.

"Will we be setting the plates," Blos asked, "like we did last year?"

"All in good time, Blos. I'll tell everyone what to do after morning announcements. Why don't you distribute these for me?"

Mr. Ho handed Blos a stack of photocopied questions. Blos counted eight questions. Eight questions Blos would have to fit into his report. Eight answers that fit those eight questions that had to fit into the report. The first bell rang. Kids were already dribbling in. Blos jumped and started running around the room distributing a page for each seat.

"Slow down, Blos," Mr. Ho said. "There's no rush."

Blos slowed down, but not much. He finished four minutes before the second bell. More students filed in. They took seats all around, none next to Blos.

Blos concentrated on his notebook. He opened it to the page he had already dated with today's date.

"You see that kid yesterday?" Ruthie Ross said.

"The one on the bleachers?" Walt Cobbler said.

"Crow," Rob Puckett said.

The kids laughed.

Who was Crow? Blos wondered.

As the late bell rang, Bethany Addams walked in.

Marjorie Howard, who usually saved her a seat, had not arrived.

"There's a place beside Blos," Mr. Ho said.

Mr. Ho always assigned Blos a partner. Bethany wrinkled her nose. She dropped her pack and sat as far away from Blos as she could.

Mr. Ho took attendance, read off the announcements, then the class stood for the Pledge of Allegiance. The class bell rang. Mr. Ho printed the topic of their latest unit, *MICROBES*, in large letters on the blackboard. Blos clicked his pen to blue and copied it down. Mr. Ho launched into a short speech about amoebas and single-celled organisms. Blos took down every word.

"We have a short lab today," Mr. Ho said. "I want you to study five slides and provide me with a full report on at least two of your choice."

There was a general rustle and hubbub as kids went to the front of the class to collect microscopes and the small boxes that held the slides. Mr. Ho continued talking.

"I would like you to cooperate with your lab partner so that each of you is doing a report on a different set of slides."

Bethany positioned the microscope and slides in front of her.

"I pick," she told Blos.

He nodded. Bethany made him feel queasy inside.

She examined all five slides first, without giving Blos a chance.

"I pick these two," she said.

She took notes and drew pictures without letting him peek at either of them.

"You get to choose from these three," she said.

She pushed the microscope and slides away from her and began working on the questions. Blos had fifteen minutes to choose and take notes. He was not good at drawing, and only getting a few minutes to sketch made it more difficult. The fifteen minutes went quickly.

The bell rang.

"Since you're still working, you can put them away," Bethany said.

Blos nodded. He glanced at his watch. He had ten minutes. Ten minutes to clean up, to put everything away, to pack up his bag, and to run down two flights of stairs, across three hallways, and make it to his seat in Ms. R's class.

Rob passed him on his way out and tapped the watch.

"Maybe Crow can teach you how to fly to classes."

"Crow?"

Rob laughed.

"Your friend at lunch yesterday."

Friend at lunch. Who did Rob mean? Lu Zimmer? Salman Page? When Blos refocused, he and Mr. Ho were alone in the classroom.

Blos fumbled with the slides. He wedged one at an angle in the slots, and it stuck, a corner sticking out. He tried pulling, pushing, took his pencil to lever it out.

Sweat beaded his forehead. His hands were slippery and wet.

A hand touched his shoulder.

"It's okay, Blos," Mr. Ho said. "Put away the microscope. I'll take care of the slides."

Blos let gratitude pour out.

"Thanks!"

He cradled the microscope in his hands and placed it next to the others on the cabinet shelf. Mr. Ho took out a pair of needle-nose pliers from a drawer and picked up the box with the wedged slide. Blos paused, surprised at the pliers. Mr. Ho gave Blos a rare smile.

"It happens almost every time. That's why I keep these on hand."

Kids from the next class were arriving, exchanging glances when they saw Blos. He ignored them. Mr. Ho had begun to unwedge the slide. Blos was fascinated by the accuracy of the pliers, the tiny motions of Mr. Ho, the slow but deliberate release of the slide. Mr. Ho looked up.

"Don't you have another class?"

Blos checked his watch. Oh no. He was going to be late. He ran all the way to Language Arts. He made it through the door just as the bell rang. He felt queasier than he had felt all morning.

"There's a seat in front," Ms. R said.

Blos crumpled into it. He heard Bethany's giggle behind him.

Blos straightened his back. He took out his notebook. Placed *A Midsummer Night's Dream* to its left. Placed his four-color pen, his pencil, his eraser, and his ruler in a line above.

"Please turn to act three, scene two," Ms. R said.

Blos turned to the page.

"Bethany, I'd like you to start at line one thirty-seven and read to us what Demetrius says when he sees Helena."

Blos heard the scramble as Bethany tried to find the lines. Then, with hesitation, she began.

*"O, Helen, goddess, nymph, perfect, divine!"*

As she read, Blos picked up his pen, clicked it to black, turned his notebook to today's date, and wrote: *A M.N.D., act 3, sc. 2.* He listened.

*". . . with the eastern wind, turns to a crow,"* Bethany read.

*Crow?* The word distracted him. Crow. It could not be Lu. She did not look anything like a crow. Maybe Salman Page? He was very dark-skinned.

"So explain: what happened to Demetrius when he saw Helena?" Ms. R asked.

Bethany had finished reading. Blos snapped back to the present. He gripped his pen tighter. He waited. Soon Ms. R was going to tell him what was meant. Soon he would write it down, word for word.

His queasiness did not return, not that whole class period.

# 7 – Lu-Ellen Zimmer

### Birds

Just before World History, Bethany Addams approached Lu. Bethany! She never spoke to Lu unless she absolutely had to.

"Crow carries worms, right? That's why birds like him."

Ruthie Ross, who sat behind Lu, piped up.

"Maybe it's 'cause his hair is shiny. Crows do go for shine."

Rob Puckett, two seats away, leaned over. "Got any birdseed for Crow?"

Bethany laughed. Lu didn't. They were talking about Salman. She shrugged.

"He's my assigned student."

This was a matter of fact. She was just a d.b. No one chose to whom they were assigned. Everyone knew that.

"Too bad you didn't get someone normal," Ruthie said.

Lu supposed that Salman didn't quite fit whatever normal was around here. But as his d.b., that didn't matter. She knew that, too. Last year, Elaine Egger had been Blos's d.b. No one called Blos normal. But Elaine was the most popular girl in school. And being Blos's d.b. had only made her popularity grow.

Lu figured she could use a little extra status, especially since Frances had moved last spring.

Frances Drummond and Lu Zimmer had been best friends since kindergarten: they had survived mean teachers together, goofed off in gym, worn each other's clothes. But last May, Frances's father's company relocated, and Memorial Day weekend, the whole family moved to Pennsylvania.

Frances had always been a little more popular than Lu—she was prettier, had blond hair, and started developing earlier. Not that Lu was ugly. But Frances was a lot more outgoing. She liked to take charge. And where Frances went, Lu followed. She was swept in whenever they did things with other kids. When Frances moved, Lu was left alone more. No one acted mean. But Lu realized too late that she had depended on Frances too much, and she wasn't really close to anyone else. She didn't have all that much in common with Frances's old crowd, except maybe for Ruthie, who played in the band with her.

Lu made up for it by calling Frances almost every day—and Frances called her back. They e-mailed and text messaged, too, but mostly they phoned. It slowed down, though. They began talking every other day, then every third or fourth. They stopped sending messages after Frances's mother joined a pool club in July and Frances made new friends. By the end of August, if they spoke once a week it was a lot. Frances's conversations were filled with "Josie this" and "Martha that." She didn't listen much to what Lu had to say.

When Lu called her last night, Frances was cold.

"Lu. What's up?"

Lu was so excited, she didn't notice the impatience in Frances's voice, not right away.

"I've become a designated buddy," Lu said. "Ms. R asked me."

"Uh-huh."

Silence dragged for a few seconds.

"Well, it's just that . . . ," Lu said.

"Hold on."

Lu heard someone in the background: "Hurry up. It's about to start."

"You have friends over." Lu faked sounding happy.

"Send me an e-mail," Frances said. "Bye."

The phone clicked in Lu's ear before she'd finished saying goodbye.

She didn't belong in Frances's life anymore. And Lu really needed someone to replace her. That's what she'd been thinking, anyway.

She put the thought aside. She was meeting Salman Page in the cafeteria. She was looking forward to that, she realized.

The first thing she noticed was his face, with every muscle clenched. He must have heard his new tag.

"There's room in the back," she said.

She didn't need to add that they wouldn't be bothered there.

Salman nodded—with effort, it seemed to her.

She found a table while Salman loaded his tray. She was trying to come up with some advice to give him, but she didn't have any. She'd never been given a tag. She watched the food line. Salman reached the cashier and handed her a pink reduced-payment slip. He paused, then walked the edge of the room, missing every group of kids that might taunt him, which Lu expected him to do. But he did it without being obvious, which was pretty awesome.

She gave him a "you go" smile. But just before he got to the table, Blos Pease showed up. Lu wondered afterward why she hadn't noticed him approach.

"May I join you?" Blos said as he sat down.

"Well . . . ," Lu said.

It's not that she disliked Blos. But Salman looked as though he needed some calm right now, and Blos would be loud and attract attention.

Salman eyed Blos before placing his tray next to Lu's bag.

"Hello, Blos," he said.

He seemed okay about Blos joining them. Okay. She could deal.

As Salman sat, Blos lined up his food, as he usually did. And when he finished lining it up, he stopped, as if something prevented him from going any further, just as he had done yesterday. He bit his lip.

"Why do they call you Crow?" he asked.

Lu tensed. Couldn't Blos, just this once, be a little tactful? She watched Salman out of the corner of her eye. She wasn't able to read his expression. He took a sip of water, set the cup down, then looked straight at Blos.

"It's because I have a crow for a friend," he said.

Blos nodded.

"I once had a pigeon for a friend," he said. "Crows are more interesting."

Blos launched himself into his lunch. Salman took another sip of water. Lu thought his eyes were smiling. She was surprised.

Blos quickly finished, crumpled up the leftovers, and crammed them into his bag. He pushed his seat back.

"Goodbye," he said.

"Do you have to be somewhere?" Salman asked.

Blos stopped.

"Uh. No. Not right away."

"Then why don't you stay with us?" Salman said.

What was he up to? Salman should have wanted him to leave. Blos was weird and tactless and had just pried into stuff Salman obviously thought was private.

Ever since Lu could remember, Blos had been apart. He attended special classes to help him socialize or something. He was smart and did well academically, but he never learned how to fit in. He took everything too literally, and he never could figure out when people were being sarcastic or were making fun of him. Lu felt sorry for him. Not that she sought him out. But she didn't avoid him the way other kids did.

Rob Puckett called him a "retard." Maybe Salman thought so, too, and planned on teasing him.

But when Salman leaned forward, she saw his face. There was no meanness there, just curiosity. Salman wanted to get to know Blos. And in a flash of insight, she saw Blos as Salman did. Blos was a boy without guile, who said what he meant and asked questions because he was curious. Lu sat back, breathing easier.

"I'd like to hear about your pigeon," Salman said, "if you don't mind."

Blos's face lit up.

"I called her Gray, because that was her color."

Salman nodded.

"How did you know that Gray was a girl?" Lu asked.

Blos grinned.

"Female pigeons are smaller than males, and their plumage is different. Besides, her eyes were so pretty, I wanted her to be a girl."

"Is she still around?" Salman asked.

Blos looked troubled.

"I have not seen her in a while. My mom says she was probably raising chicks in a quiet place."

"She was your friend, though," Salman said.

Blos nodded vigorously.

"I fed her and talked to her, and when it froze last winter, I opened the storm window and set up a box against the inside window, with rags and paper, so she would not be so cold."

"Did she use it?" Lu asked.

"Oh yes. Until the spring—when it warmed up."

"She'll come back," Salman said.

"You really think so?" Blos said.

Salman nodded again. "You have a warm roost."

"And I will not roast her," Blos said.

It was a bad pun, poorly executed. But Salman laughed a quiet laugh that made his eyes crinkle. Pleased, Blos guffawed in his too-loud way. Lu had to smile, too.

Blos checked his watch.

"I have to go."

He rushed off.

Salman frowned. "We have at least ten more minutes."

"He likes to be early," Lu said.

Blos had a thing about schedules. He constantly worried about being late, consulting his oversized watch at every occasion. He was first in line for everything.

Salman took a bite out of his pizza. Lu nibbled on her egg salad sandwich. She didn't have much appetite.

"Why'd you tell him about your crow?" she asked.

"I call him Bird."

He almost sounded like Blos.

"Okay. So how come you told him about Bird?"

"Because he'll keep it to himself."

"How do you know?"

Salman grinned. "He never told you about Gray, did he?"

She shook her head. Salman was right. Blos never had.

"He'll keep it to himself," Salman said.

She sipped her milk. She had known Blos since first grade. And here Salman had understood him better than she did. Impressive.

"Do you like Blos?" she asked.

Salman nodded. "I've met kids like him before."

"Really?"

Salman hesitated. "In other schools. Other kids are like him. I've sat with them, sometimes." He paused, then added, "Blos is real. What you see is what you get."

No hidden agendas. No plans to hurt you. Salman

didn't say those words, but Lu knew that's what he meant.

"Yes," she said. "That's him."

Salman was getting ready to leave. She didn't want to let him go. Not yet. She wondered what else he might see that she didn't.

"What do you have this afternoon?"

"A lab with Mr. Ho."

"Your first?" she asked.

Salman nodded.

"Writing his reports is a real pain," Lu said.

Salman stared, questioning.

"He makes you rewrite them until he thinks you've done it right."

Salman frowned. An eyebrow furrowed down. She could tell he didn't like that idea.

"I can show you how he expects them to be done," she said. "If you want."

"Okay," Salman said.

He appeared relieved.

"We can work at my house," she said.

The eyebrow began to furrow again.

"It's only a few blocks away, and Mom can drive you home."

Salman glanced out the windows. Rain pelted against them. He seemed to be calculating something in his head.

"Okay. But I'll need to be back at my place for dinner."

"No problem," she said.

She watched him walk away. With his right hand he slipped his tray onto the rollers by the kitchen window, while with the left he lifted the cutlery and dropped it into the plastic tub. In the next stride he swooped up his backpack by the entrance and was gone.

Graceful. He reminded her of a shortstop making a play during one of the many baseball games she had watched with her dad. A good shortstop.

She dumped her bag into the trash and was retrieving her pack when she noticed Rob Puckett talking to one of his crew. They had been watching Salman, and Rob said something to make the other boy giggle.

Her stomach turned cold all of a sudden.

# 8

## Dreams

Salman Page
September _____
Language Arts

TOPIC: Write about a dream and what it told you.

    I dreamed I became a bird.
    I was sitting in the crook of a tree, and my mind was busy—full of what was happening to me every day where I live now. Then, somehow, I became a crow that had just taken off. I saw myself, Salman the boy, small, nestled in the

tree, and I saw trees all around, other birds flying, and people far below, and I caught a glint out of the corner of my eye. I dove for the glint—a bottle cap shining in a parking lot—scooped it up, and flew away to the tallest tree, not too far from that tiny boy on the branch. And I dropped my treasure into a little hollow, heard it clink as it joined my other treasures, and I cawed with pleasure. How did I become this bird?

Dreams are so thin that they evaporate in daylight. Yet after I woke from my dream, it stayed with me. I felt it, inside me. And the next time a crow flew by, swooped, and cawed, I once again saw myself, small and straight, hand on my forehead to shield the bright sun, a speck compared to the world that the bird soared around in. How did I see this?

Some say dreams are the product of a person's mind when it has nothing else to do. Maybe. But maybe dreams are a bit of magic, allowing us to be something else, somewhere else, for a while, so you can see and hear what others feel. That's what my dream told me.

# 9–Salman Page

### Mr. Ho likes graph paper

At the top of Salman's essay, Ms. R had written *very good* in red ink. Salman might have been pleased except for the words added in blue ink: *Please see me at the end of class.*

What did Ms. R want? He had let himself slip again: he had revealed too much of himself, writing this essay.

Salman approached the teacher's desk after the bell rang. He hoped she wouldn't keep him too long. He was supposed to meet Lu by the front entrance. They were going to go over his lab report for Mr. Ho.

"Your writing is remarkable," Ms. R said.

Salman didn't reply. "Remarkable" might mean something good. It might mean something bad.

"How old are you, Salman?" Ms. R asked.

"Fourteen."

Turning fifteen next month, he thought.

Ms. R nodded as if that explained everything.

Now Salman felt embarrassed. It wasn't his fault he had been held back. Each new foster home had meant a new school. Somehow, in third and again in fifth grade, he hadn't accumulated the right number of days he needed to be moved up. He briefly wondered how many days he'd lose this year when the state switched him again.

What *did* this teacher want?

"Would you like to write for the school paper?" she asked.

Salman wasn't prepared for the question. He stalled. "What do you have to do?"

"Write an article about once a month. The topics are pretty wide open. They usually have to do with something relating to the school."

Once a month. Salman didn't think he was going to be around that long—not if Ozzy had any say about it.

"No thanks," he said.

"Well, think about it," Ms. R said. "I think you'd be good at it."

Would he be good at it? After all, his first foster mother had named him Salman after a famous writer. He pushed the unwanted thought aside.

He met Lu amidst a stream of other students at the

foot of the main staircase. Her huge backpack weighed her down, as usual. She waved at another girl who was walking away and yelled at her over the din, "See you at band, Ruthie!"

Lu turned to Salman. She bubbled as she spoke.

"Ms. R asked me to join the paper today."

Salman nodded. They headed toward the entrance. "Me too."

Lu stopped. A couple of kids almost bumped into her. "No way! That's great!"

Rob Puckett passed them with two other boys.

"Hey, look," he said, loud. "It's Crow. And he's got his bird tamer with him."

Several kids turned to see whom Rob was talking about. The two boys laughed. Lu ducked her head down.

"Let's go."

The front doors were blocked by a large group of kids who hesitated before rain cascading down the front steps. Lu and Salman exchanged glances.

"It's only two blocks," Lu said.

Salman nodded. They pushed through and began running almost simultaneously.

At Lu's house, they shook themselves out on the porch. Salman thought they must look like a pair of wet dogs. Lu's bobbed hair had matted to her skull and it dripped all over. A rivulet trickled down Salman's back.

Ms. Zimmer met them at the door. She seemed unfazed by the new kid on her doorstep.

"You don't come in until you take off your shoes and socks," she said.

The command had been good-natured. Salman unlaced his soaked sneakers and pulled off his socks. Ms. Zimmer handed Lu and Salman towels.

"Lu, go upstairs and change," she said.

"This is Salman," Lu said before climbing the stairs.

Ms. Zimmer turned to Salman. He was struck by how beautiful she was. Tall, with green eyes and curly red hair pulled back into a messy ponytail, she glowed, not the least bit abashed by her enormous pregnant belly. Salman averted his gaze.

"Lu's your something-or-other buddy?" she said.

"Designated," Salman said, his voice just over a whisper.

Her eyes narrowed.

"You're a bit slimmer than Ronny, but I think I can find something. Stay put."

She, too, climbed the stairs. As ordered, Salman stayed put while he eyed his strange surroundings—and wondered who Ronny might be.

Compared to the Royals' trailer, this house was huge. The furniture, or at least what he saw of it, appeared ragtag, and no curtains or blinds hid the windows.

A tall teenage boy, taller than Salman, stepped out of a door, biting into an apple.

"Who are you?" he demanded.

"A friend of Lu's." Salman felt odd saying this. He

wasn't exactly her friend. But, after a quick up-and-down appraisal, the boy seemed satisfied with the explanation.

"You look soaked."

Well, d-uh, Salman thought. But from experience, he knew that if he didn't want trouble, he was better off being polite.

"Ms. Zimmer told me to wait here."

The boy raised an eyebrow.

"Mom has—"

He was interrupted by Ms. Zimmer.

"Jack. Good, you've met Salman. Please show him a bathroom. He can change into these."

Jack didn't seem at all surprised that his mother planned to give clothes to a complete stranger. He grabbed the sweatpants and shirt and, with a tilt of his head, had Salman follow him through the living room, into a narrow hallway.

"The bathroom's through that door," he said.

The sweatshirt and pants were baggy but dry. When Salman returned to the front hall, Lu was waiting.

"I'll put your stuff in the dryer," she said.

Salman had forgotten that people owned dryers—almost all of the homes he had ever lived in didn't have one. He handed his wet clothes to her and followed her into the kitchen. Ms. Zimmer smiled when she saw them.

"Have a snack."

He took in the unfamiliar scene. Ms. Zimmer poured herself a glass of milk while a boy no older than nine or ten ate handfuls of popcorn out of a large serving bowl. Fruit overflowed from a second bowl on the table. Another boy—around sixteen, Salman guessed—just about Salman's height, leaned against the counter. He was dressed all in white, with sewed-on white knee pads and chest plate. He reminded Salman of a spaceman from a bad sci-fi movie. Lu disappeared at the other end of the room with Salman's clothes.

Ms. Zimmer made introductions.

"Salman, these are Lu's other brothers, Ronny and Ricky."

The spaceboy smiled.

"Call me Ron," he said.

Ricky stuffed another handful of popcorn into his mouth.

Salman managed a "hi."

Ms. Zimmer glanced at the clock over the stove and put the barely drunk glass of milk on the counter.

"We'd better leave," she said.

Ron picked up a white helmet with a mesh face and followed her out the back door. Salman stared.

"Fencing," Ricky said between mouthfuls.

"What?"

"That's what you wanted to know, right?"

"I guess," Salman said.

He now understood what it must be like to be an alien dropped into a new world. He needed to adjust, fast. At that moment Lu reappeared.

"Going to show your boyfriend around?" Ricky said.

Lu rolled her eyes.

"Any objections?" she said.

It took a second for Salman to recognize the sarcasm in her tone—he somehow hadn't expected it from her.

"Don't touch any of my airplanes," Ricky said.

Lu let out a small laugh.

"We'll try." She turned to Salman. "Let's go to the study. It'll be quieter there."

Lu transferred some of the popcorn into a smaller bowl, which she handed to Salman. Ricky nabbed the few kernels that spilled onto the table. She reshouldered her pack and led Salman down a hallway. She pointed to a door on the right.

"Guest room," she said.

She turned left through another door. This must be the study.

Salman had never seen a study before, but even so, the room looked like one. Books filled the walls. A desk stood on one side of the room, a sofa on the other, and a table with a couple of chairs in the middle. He hadn't noticed any airplanes yet.

"This used to be my dad's work space," Lu said, "until he moved his office into town."

Salman wondered what Lu's father did but didn't ask. The room was peaceful. He breathed in, and out. Adjusting to this place wasn't going to be so hard.

Lu took the popcorn from him to place it on the table and dropped her backpack on a chair. She waved to the bowl.

"Have some," she said.

Salman helped himself while Lu unzipped her pack.

"Crap! Everything got wet."

She pulled out several books and notebooks with wilted edges. One of the notebooks slipped out of her hands and fell. Salman reached for it. Lu smiled when he handed it to her. That smile lodged itself somewhere in his chest. He smiled back. She spread the notebook next to the others on the desk to dry.

Salman checked his pack. All he carried in it were his math textbook and his binder. He didn't own any notebooks. Ozzy Royal wouldn't buy him any.

"Loose-leaf works just as well," the man had said.

The binder's plastic cover had protected Salman's papers. He turned to his lab notes.

Lu leaned over. "How'd you fit it all on half a page—including your sketches?"

Salman didn't reply. He wrote small. He was allowed only a few sheets of paper at a time: Ozzy kept tabs on his stack.

"Let Salman be," Tina had said. "It's for school."

But Salman didn't waste any space or paper. He had learned that lesson well before meeting Ozzy. Even his last foster mother, Ms. D, told him, "No need writing things down all the time. Keep the paper for assignments." So when he did get a sheet of paper, he used every bit of it, carefully.

Lu sat at the table.

"Did Mr. Ho give you an outline?" she said.

Salman showed her the photocopied sheet Mr. Ho had distributed: it listed ten questions about the worm dissection they had completed.

"I follow this?" he asked.

Lu shook her head.

"Nah. He doesn't make it that easy. I'll show you."

She took a blank page from Salman's binder. He tried not to wince. She paused.

"Mr. Ho likes graph paper. Do you have any?"

Salman frowned. He didn't have any, and Ozzy wasn't going to buy him any, either. But that didn't deter Lu.

"You can use some of ours."

She opened a desk drawer, pulled out a pad, and tore off a bunch of sheets, which she held out to Salman. He stared at them. After a few seconds, Lu placed them on the table.

"Take them. They don't bite."

"I can't pay you back," Salman said.

Lu shrugged him off.

"Don't worry about it. It's just a few pages."

Salman did have to worry about it. He counted the pages. There were three of them.

"Thanks," he said.

For the next hour and a half, Lu showed him how to divide up the topics, where the drawings were supposed to be placed, even the size of the margins.

About halfway through, they paused to eat more popcorn. He felt comfortable enough to ask the question that had been bothering him since they had left the kitchen.

"What airplanes was your brother talking about?"

Lu frowned, but her eyes crinkled with amusement.

"Paper airplanes," she said. "Ricky's been experimenting with designs."

She told him how he had left dozens strewn all over the house until their mom had warned him that if he didn't clean up, she was going to use them to light a fire in the grate.

Lu must have noticed Salman's horror because she stopped to reassure him.

"Oh, Mom wouldn't have done it. But it did get Ricky to store 'em in his room."

Salman nodded.

"There's still a few around, though," she added, laughter in her voice. "Dad got pretty annoyed when one showed up in the bathroom."

Salman imagined a paper plane marooned in a sink and grinned. They returned to work.

When he finished the report, it fit onto both sides of one sheet of paper.

"Wow," Lu said. "I usually use four pages."

Salman didn't explain.

He was placing his binder in his pack when Ms. Zimmer stepped in, her skirt damp around the hem.

"Will you stay for dinner, Salman? We eat in about an hour, when Lu's father gets home from work."

Salman glanced at the clock on the desk. It was already five o'clock.

"I need to head back," he said. "They're expecting me."

"I'll give you a ride, then."

Salman's clothes, now dry, hung on the back of a kitchen chair. They felt scratchy after the soft fleece of the sweats. Ms. Zimmer insisted that Salman borrow Ron's old slicker.

"Just got you dry," she said. "No point in letting you get wet."

Her generosity, genuine in every way, warmed him. He left the slicker in the van before dashing into the trailer.

Tina and Ozzy didn't ask Salman where he had been. After Salman dropped his pack in his bedroom, Tina told him to set the table. Ozzy stood at the window, beer can in hand, watching Ms. Zimmer back up the driveway. He returned to his TV.

"Nice van," he said.

Salman sighed. Nice people.

# 10–Puck

### No particular grace

My king waylaid me after my audience with the queen. He had conjured an image of the boy sitting on an invisible chair and eating. He pointed at the image.

"He is no small child," he said.

"No, milord."

The king glared at the boy. "Why does she insist on following this human? She knows my opinion of him."

Of course Queen Titania did. She had given him up as an infant only after the king, in a fit of jealousy, had forced her to. That is precisely why I had been given this thankless task. The queen wished to provoke my king. To get back at him for having visited Nimue's island over her objections. (Curse, curse, and curse again the circlet!) She followed the boy because she knew how angry it would make the king.

But this answer wouldn't please my queen if I spoke it. And my king's rage, in turn, would be too dangerous to bear. I decided on a blander truth.

"My queen told the boy's mother, before her death, that she would keep the boy safe until he reached manhood."

King Oberon brushed that aside. "So Titania says. Yet she has ignored him since he was a babe, swaddled in his foster mother's arms. And look at him! He's on the cusp of manhood. Not the least bit pleasing to her eye!"

I bowed. There was no good reply. The king paced, his words forceful.

"I have had enough of this. The boy does not deserve her attention!"

He dismissed the image with a wave. The queen would be happy when she heard of his anger, I thought.

"If she is so eager to keep track of this whelp, perhaps I should give her something to keep track of."

I did not like the sound of this.

"Milord?"

"Tell me what you have learned."

The queen had not forbidden me, and so I had to report. But fear tinged my words.

"One of the queen's namesakes cares for him, milord."

He raised an eyebrow.

"Titania Royal," I said. "But she has none of Her Majesty's grace and beauty."

"That could not be expected in a human, Puck. But this bodes ill. The name carries gifts of its own."

I agreed. "She is extremely bountiful."

"Bountiful?"

"Her garden is prodigious," I explained.

Oberon nodded again. "Tell me more."

"Her mate broods and imbibes."

The king seemed pleased with that, so I clarified, "But she is his equal—she protects the boy."

He paced again, thinking. "I cannot strike at his home. To do so would provoke outright war with Titania." He stopped pacing. "Does the boy have any companions?"

"Two scholars, milord."

"Conjure them."

I did. The king walked around the silent, moving figures.

"Tell me about them."

"The young man is both like and unlike us."

Oberon paused his perpetual motion.

"Like and unlike? Could he be a changeling, one of Faery?"

I shook my head. "He is human. I am certain. But he sees the world as it is and not as humans would have it be."

"This is a strange gift. What of the other?"

"A mentor, Your Majesty. She is helpful."

Oberon looked at her carefully. "No particular grace. Yet her eyes show intelligence. Her limbs, strength and musical ability. Her face is comely in its way. She will grow into a fine figure. Does the boy grow fond of her, Puck?"

"He may."

The truth. But it only increased King Oberon's interest.

"Well, well." He snapped his fingers and the images vanished.

"You have reported this all to the queen?"

I bowed.

"Yes, milord."

"And she approves?"

A direct question that required a direct answer.

"Yes, milord."

"And has she given you instructions?"

I remained impassive. I had to.

"To continue my observations."

King Oberon smiled.

"Of course. Now tell me, Puck, tell me true. Are there any in the girl's circle of acquaintances whom you have influence over?"

This was a cruel question. Everyone has influence somewhere—it is our private joy and power. To be forced to disclose it . . . Only a sovereign can demand it, and only from his vassal. I bowed my head, hiding the resentment that must have shone in my eyes.

"Among the scholars. There is a boy."

"Not the ungainly one you conjured?"

I shook my head.

"Who then?"

"A certain Robin Puckett."

"Ah."

He rubbed his hands.

"You must sow discord, Puck."

Finally! A way out.

"I cannot, milord. I am bound to protect the boy. My queen has demanded it."

"Of course," the king said. "But you are not bound to protect the girl."

No! How was I to explain any of this to the queen?

"Visit this Robin Puckett's dreams, Puck. Visit his dreams!"

And as I watched the king disappear, I cursed my position.

# 11 – Lu-Ellen Zimmer

### Waterfalls

Dinner at Lu's house was noisy. Everyone talked at the same time, her brothers vying for Mom and Dad's attention. Lu usually tuned out. She lived in a house full of boys. Everything was about sports and video games and Jack's acting and Ron's fencing and Ricky's latest boy genius project—when he wasn't just being a total pain. Salman seemed different.

Lu picked at her food. Salman was nice—a loner and a bit weird, but definitely nice. Older, too, she guessed. He looked like someone Ron's age. And Bird—well, he was magical.

She frowned. Kids were calling Salman "Crow."

She bit her lip and began to build a hill of peas on

one side of her plate. This wasn't about her, she reminded herself. She was only his d.b. Salman was a strong kid. He'd weather it. She squashed some of the peas, and one rolled off the plate. As she leaned over to retrieve it, she realized Mom was speaking to her.

". . . tomorrow evening. It'll be nice to see them."

"Tomorrow evening?" Lu said.

"We're meeting the Drummonds," Mom said. "I was speaking to Natalie. . . ."

She stared at Lu.

"Haven't you been listening?"

Lu reddened. Natalie? Frances Drummond's mother? They were meeting the Drummonds?

"She's dreaming about her new boyfriend," Ricky said.

Lu wanted to kick him, but he was across the table, too far to reach. Dad's fork stopped halfway to his mouth.

"Boyfriend?"

Oh great. She had better put a stop to this, fast.

"I'm a designated buddy," Lu said. "I showed my buddy how to write a report for Mr. Ho."

Dad nodded.

"Seems like a nice boy," Mom said.

He is, Lu thought.

"What were you saying about the Drummonds?" she asked.

"I spoke to Natalie this morning. She and the girls will be in town. We arranged to meet for dinner."

Dinner. Dinner with Frances's mother and the girls—that meant Frances and her little sister, Johanna.

"The whole family's going to have dinner with them?" Lu asked.

"No. Just you and me."

Lu and Mom. No brothers. This sounded good.

"No fair," Ricky said. "I wanna come, too."

"You have soccer practice, young man," Dad said.

Go, Dad!

"And who's gonna take me?"

"I've made arrangements with Jimmy Puckett's mother," Mom said. "You can ride with them."

"It still isn't fair—"

Jack interrupted. "Mom, can I sign you up for the costume committee?"

Chaos resumed. Mom and Jack talked about the high school play. Ricky, still mad, began whining about how mean his soccer coach was. Ron chose this moment to ask Dad whether he could purchase a new fencing foil.

"What's wrong with the one you used last year?" Dad said.

"Well . . ."

Lu let her thoughts wander. Dinner with Frances. She should be more excited. Two weeks ago, she would have been. But now she wondered what she'd tell Frances. And what Frances had to say. Should Lu mention Salman? What about his crow?

✽ ✽ ✽

When Lu got to school the next morning, she saw Rob Puckett and a bunch of other guys snickering as they climbed the stairs. She would have ignored them, except that Rob caught her eye and gave her an evil smile. She was halfway to her homeroom when she ran into Salman, his mouth drawn into a tight frown.

"What's up?" she asked.

He hesitated before pulling a sheet of paper from his pack: a picture printed off the Internet. A dead crow's body lay splayed on the ground.

"Found it on my locker," he said.

Why were they picking on Salman? Then later, during math class, Bethany Addams sent her a note.

*You like him, don't you.*

What had she done to Bethany?

When Lu searched for Ruthie at lunch, hoping to get some explanation from her, she found her in deep conversation with Bethany. Lu headed to the back of the cafeteria, behind a post. Best she let this blow over, she figured.

By the end of the day, she had almost forgotten the note. She had begun thinking about her assignments for tomorrow, and how little time she had to complete them, when Rob ambushed her on the way to the front doors.

"Hello, Bird Tamer," he said.

Sean, a heavyset boy, blocked her path.

"Get out of my way," she said.

"If you show us how you tamed Crow," Rob said.

She glared at him. What kind of idiocy was this? Kids were streaming past. At that moment Blos Pease ran up, on his way to the bus line.

"Hey, Lu. Ms. R said I can work for the paper."

Blos didn't seem to notice Rob and Sean, who were now smirking.

"I wanted to tell you at lunch but I did not see you."

"That's great, Blos," Lu said.

Blos checked his watch. "The bus loads in five minutes. Bye."

He dove between Lu and the boys, aiming for the line, forcing the boys aside. Lu grabbed her chance and ran out the doors before they could corner her again. She'd have to thank Blos sometime for having helped her.

But she didn't have time to dwell on it. She spent every minute at home trying to finish all of her homework.

"We're leaving!" Mom yelled from the stairs.

"Be right there!" Lu yelled back.

She fished out a light sweater from her closet to wear over her T-shirt.

During the fifteen-minute ride to the restaurant, she tried to calm her jitters. She was having dinner with Frances. Their last conversation hadn't been great, but they were still friends—at least, Lu hoped so. Maybe this was their chance to work out whatever distance had crept between them and get back to the friendship they used to have.

At the diner, Frances, her mother, and her seven-year-old sister, Johanna, waved from a circular booth as soon as Lu and Mom walked in. Lu gave Frances a shy smile. Frances smiled back. Natalie—she was *never* to be called Ms. Drummond—rose and hugged Mom.

"Marianne, you look fabulous!"

Fabulous? Natalie—with her blond hair cut straight just over her shoulders, tasteful makeup, silk shirt and crisp trousers fitted to her slim frame, and a gold necklace with a large blue stone that matched her eyes— exuded fabulous. Mom, on the other hand, wore no makeup; ringlets of red hair escaped her ponytail; and she had on one of Dad's dress shirts over preggie pants— "because they fit," she had explained. Something of a mess, Lu thought.

They sat themselves around the table, Lu next to Frances. Johanna sat between the two moms.

"Hi," Lu said.

"Hi," Frances replied.

A split second of awkwardness was interrupted by Mom.

"Tell me about your house."

"It's beautiful, Marianne," Natalie said. "Everything we ever wanted."

That wasn't what Lu had heard.

When Frances had first moved in, she complained that the house was cold. Built among ginormous homes on two-acre lots, the Drummond house was just like the rest: too big with fourteen rooms and a three-car garage.

"They forgot to give the place a soul," Frances had said. "I feel like I live in a fancy furniture catalog."

"It can't be that bad," Lu had said.

"It's worse. I keep on expecting someone to tell me it's closing time and I need to leave the showroom so they can lock up."

They had laughed over the phone.

But now Frances was nodding at her mother's glowing description.

"We put a pool in next spring," Natalie said.

Johanna squirmed. "I want lemonade," she said.

"We'll order in a minute," Natalie replied.

Lu rolled her eyes at Frances. Johanna was acting just like Ricky. Frances rolled her eyes back. "Little sisters," she was saying. They both giggled.

"The furniture—" Natalie began.

"Can I have chicken fingers?" Johanna interrupted.

"When we order," Natalie said.

Lu gave a tiny shake of her head, so that only Frances noticed.

"It's almost like home," Lu said.

"Is Ricky still blowing things up?" Frances asked.

"He's moved to floods."

"Naw . . ."

"You should have seen the kitchen after he built his wave machine."

Frances grinned in anticipation.

Lu described how Ricky had cut up almost all of the plastic containers Mom used for leftovers and had connected them with duct tape to make one long basin. Then he built a tall frame over one end, and from it hung a piece of wood into the basin.

"He filled the contraption with water and a few boats and then started pushing the piece of wood back and forth."

"Did it make waves?" Frances asked.

"Oh yeah," Lu said. "Beautiful big ones."

Even Johanna's eyes, at this point, were dancing. "Did it make a mess?" she asked.

"Only when the waves broke over the sides," Mom said.

Lu began giggling.

"And then . . . the duct tape . . . sprung a leak. . . ."

Frances, too, began laughing.

"He had waterfalls going off the ends of the table," Lu finished.

"His next experiment," Mom said, "was with a mop."

Lu grinned.

"Now he's into paper airplanes."

"Everywhere," Mom said, waving her hands.

Natalie dabbed a tissue at the corners of her eyes.

"I don't know how you manage, Marianne," she said.

"Four children over ten. Jack about to graduate high school. And now a baby on the way . . ."

Mom's smile tightened.

"I feel fortunate carrying another child."

"Of course you do!" Natalie said.

What she meant, Lu understood, was "Better you than me."

Mom steered the conversation back to Natalie's choice of furniture. The waiter arrived and took their dinner orders.

"Tell me about your classes," Lu said to Frances.

While they ate, Mom and Natalie chatted about upholstery, the state of education, the gardens they had planted. Johanna chimed in with her opinions. Lu and Frances talked about old acquaintances.

After ordering dessert, Frances said, "You mentioned you were a designated buddy."

Lu froze. The dinner had been pleasant so far, even warm. Their old friendship had returned, little by little, although not completely. They had skipped past being polite with one another but still hadn't revealed much about themselves. How much did she dare tell Frances, especially with their mothers and Frances's sister overhearing every word?

But Frances had remembered. She had paid attention during that short phone call when Lu thought she had been distracted.

"The kid's a nice guy," Lu said. "He's new to Spring-falls."

"What do you do with him?"

"I've shown him stuff around the school."

"Oh?"

"Well, yesterday, for example, I showed him how to write a biology report for Mr. Ho so he wouldn't have to do it twice."

Lu and Frances had labored over Mr. Ho's reports together last year.

"That's really nice," Frances said.

She had said it as if she meant it. Lu had her opening. She could tell Frances about Salman's tiny hand-writing. She could mention how raggedy his clothes were and speculate whether he picked them out or didn't have a choice. She could talk about his crow.

But no, she realized, she couldn't. She wasn't ready to talk about Salman. Not with Frances. Not right now.

"Does your school have designated buddies?" she asked.

Frances sighed.

"I wish it did. Those first few weeks were really tough."

They moved safely away from Salman. Soon, it was time to go. Frances took Lu's arm in hers as they walked behind their mothers and Johanna toward the cars.

The night was clear and cold. Even under the city

lights, Lu saw a few stars and the quarter moon. Beautiful, she thought.

"Did you see that dress?" Frances said.

She pointed to a display in the store next to the diner. A headless mannequin wore a glitzy gown with at least three bows too many.

"Frilly," Lu said.

"Martha'd have a field day," Frances said. She began laughing. "You should have heard her talking about all the dresses after the summer ball at the pool club. She had me and Josie in stitches."

Lu smiled, but only halfheartedly.

They reached Frances's car first.

"Take it easy, okay?" Frances said.

"Okay," Lu said.

Frances gave her a real hug. Lu hugged her back.

As she watched them drive away, Lu shivered in her light sweater.

# 12 – Blos Pease

### Feathers

Blos remembered when Frances Drummond moved away. She had been Lu Zimmer's best friend, and whenever he saw Lu at school, he knew that Frances was probably nearby. Frances always made him feel queasy inside. So he never stayed around Lu for very long. Except sometimes Lu ate lunch with him—with him and their d.b., Elaine Egger—without Frances. He never felt queasy then. Lu always said hi. And after Frances moved away, he could say hi back and not worry that Frances was going to show up and make him feel queasy inside.

What Blos really liked about Lu was that she never told Blos things she knew were not true. Not like Rob Puckett. Rob Puckett always told Blos lies.

Just before first period, Rob had told him, "Your feathers are showing!"

The other kids laughed. Blos did not. He did not have any feathers on him. His mother bought him a down jacket last winter. Down was a kind of feather that trapped air very well and kept you warm. It was the only thing with feathers he owned. But the weather had not been cold enough to wear his down jacket. He could not have had *any* feathers on him.

He told his mother at dinner, "Rob Puckett said, 'Your feathers are showing,' but I did not have any feathers."

"No," she said. "You didn't."

"The other kids laughed."

Mom let out a big breath. She did that sometimes.

"It's one of the things you have to ignore."

"Lu Zimmer had feathers."

"Oh?"

That morning, a whole lot of feathers stuck out of Lu's locker. Blos had seen them when he was storing his lunch bag.

"She took them out of her locker and put them in the trash."

Blos was not sure why Mom nodded. Maybe she thought that feathers belonged in the trash, too.

"Do you see Lu a lot?"

"Mostly at lunch. Maybe for the school paper."

They were going to have their first school paper

meeting Friday morning, half an hour before the first bell. Yesterday, Mom had promised to give him a ride.

"You sit with Lu at lunch?"

"Yes. Her and Salman Page."

He had told Mom about Salman, the very day he had met him. Salman was from Bridgeport.

Mom was smiling. Blos knew that was a good thing.

"I like it when I have lunch with her," Blos said.

"I like it, too," Mom said.

Blos was not sure why he had said that to Mom, but it was true. Lunches with Lu were good days. Even last year, before Frances Drummond had moved away, when Elaine Egger was their d.b. Lunches were even better now because Salman was there, too.

The next day he saw Lu and Salman all the way across the cafeteria.

"Hi!" he called.

He rushed over and put his food on the table. But just as he began sorting his food, Salman spoke up.

"Lu says you're joining the paper. Is that right?"

His food lay all over the place, the carrots perched over the cookies, the eggs under the rolls, and the sliced apple off to the side. Mom had told him, "When someone speaks to you, you have to acknowledge him or her." So he nodded first, then quickly put everything in its place before answering, "Ms. R said I can take pictures."

Blos was worried. What if Salman asked him another

question and he had to answer that one, too? He eyed his food. It needed to be eaten. And Mom had told him, "Don't talk with your mouth full." He had trouble with that rule, so they worked it out so that he only talked after he ate his meal. But this was school. What if Blos had to eat and speak at the same time?

"It's okay," Salman said. "Have your lunch."

Blos was relieved. Salman even waited until he had finished before asking him his next question. Like Mom.

"You have a camera?"

"Digital," Blos said. "It is brand new."

Mom had given it to him a week ago, for his birthday.

"Really?" Salman said.

"I like new things."

"Have you taken any pictures yet?" Lu asked.

"Two," Blos said.

"Can we see them sometime?"

Blos panicked. The pictures were still in the camera. And Mom had said he had to be careful with the camera, so he was not supposed to bring it to school unless he needed to use it for official school paper business. Mom had agreed to that. But there was no paper business today.

"I—I have to print them . . . print them out. . . ."

"Only if you want to," Lu said.

He wanted to. The pictures were of his mother in their living room, and the front of his house—the ones he took when his mom asked him to test the camera.

They were not bad pictures. But, he thought, Ms. R had told him to take many pictures for the school paper so they could pick out the best one. He needed more pictures. Yes. If he took more pictures, he could show those to Lu, too.

He checked his watch. Just two more periods before he could go home, take more pictures, and print them out.

"Okay," Blos said. "Goodbye."

# 13 – Lu-Ellen Zimmer

### Whistles

Lu wondered why Blos ran off as soon as they asked him about his camera. Even after all these years, she didn't always understand why he did some things.

"Did I say something wrong?"

"No," Salman said. "I don't think so."

But she could see that Salman's mind was someplace else. He stared out the windows at the beautiful fall day: crisp, a slight breeze, clear blue skies.

"Would you like to do homework at my house this afternoon?" she asked.

"Not today." Then, as an afterthought, he added, "Thanks."

The lunch bell rang. Lu dumped her bag into the trash and Salman glided away. She leaned over to pick up her backpack when she noticed a small brown paper bag wedged in her strap.

She checked over her shoulder. No one was watching her—at least, no one she could see. She opened the bag. Inside was a metal whistle and a folded sheet of paper. Letters, cut out from magazines, were pasted into a note.

*To call your birds.*

She crumpled the paper and reddened. The note had been unsigned, but she knew who had left her the whistle.

As she headed toward the stairs, Rob Puckett and Sean surprised her.

"Let's hear it blow," Sean called, and Rob let out a wolf whistle.

Lu ran to class. A cold ball froze her gut that entire afternoon. What had she done to get on their hit list?

She was so upset, she kept flubbing her part at band practice. Ruthie tried to help, but Ms. Cantor lost patience.

"Lu, you need to spend more time practicing!"

When Lu arrived home, she realized she had left the play they were reading for Language Arts in her locker. She didn't worry, though. Her parents owned so many books, she was sure they must have a copy of it somewhere in the house. Finding it, however, was another story. Whatever system Dad had created to shelve the books never made sense to her.

Lu found Mom in the kitchen, pouring juice for Ricky.

"Do we have a copy of *A Midsummer Night's Dream*?" she asked.

Mom handed Ricky the glass.

"I think so. I'll check the study. What do you need it for?"

"Homework."

"So you can tell your boyfriend about it when you see him?" Ricky said.

"No, twit. Go find someone else to bother."

"It bothers you that you have a boyfriend?"

"I *don't* have a boyfriend! Will you leave me alone?"

"Jimmy Puckett's brother says you hang around with *two* boys. Maybe you can't make up your mind."

"Mom. Can you tell Ricky to shut up?"

Mom's eyes crinkled, as if she were smiling.

"Ricky, leave your sister alone. You have homework to do."

Lu followed Mom into the study. Mom leaned behind the couch and pulled out a few books.

"Here it is," she said. She huffed as she straightened. Lu took *The Riverside Shakespeare* from her—a big, heavy volume.

"Everything he wrote is there," Mom said.

Lu riffled the pages. She found the play on page 217—at the very beginning of the book. Jeez. She placed the open volume on the table. Mom stood beside her.

"Are you okay, honey? You seem upset about something."

"Ricky drives me crazy."

Mom grinned. "Well, yes. That's his job."

"No, it isn't!"

Mom laughed. "Every younger sibling drives the older siblings a bit crazy. Even you did."

"I never went on and on the way he does."

"Maybe," Mom said.

Mom didn't move. Why didn't she leave Lu alone?

"Is something else bothering you?" Mom asked.

Well, yes. School. This must have been one of the worst days of her life. Lu was used to not being on the most popular list. But being singled out by the likes of Rob Puckett and Bethany Addams was entirely new. She fingered the onionskin-thin pages of the book. She wondered what Mom'd say if she told her some kids were calling her Bird Tamer. Maybe she'd laugh about that, too. Lu glanced up. Mom was smiling—an inviting smile. No, Lu had to admit, she wouldn't laugh.

Mom placed a hand on her belly and winced. She seemed paler than usual.

"Are you okay?" Lu asked.

"The baby thinks my bladder makes a great trampoline."

Ouch, Lu thought.

"But what about you?" Mom said. "You seem a bit sad to me."

"I'm okay," Lu said. Mom had enough to worry about.

"We can talk if you want," Mom said.

Lu nodded and looked back down at the book.

"I'm okay."

As Lu lugged the volume upstairs, Ron almost slammed into her on his way down.

"I'm late," he said.

He crashed his way to the kitchen, yelling, "Mom! Can you give me a ride?"

Ricky had turned on the TV, despite Mom's instructions about homework. Jack had music blaring from his room. With all the noise, Lu didn't hear the phone ring.

"Lu!" Ron yelled from downstairs.

Lu stuck her head over the stairwell.

"Call for you!" he yelled.

She dumped the book onto her desk and grabbed the receiver. She waited for the telltale click that the phone downstairs had been hung up before talking.

"Hello?"

"Hi, Lu. It's Frances. I have great news!"

Frances. Yes! Someone to talk to. Lu felt a moment of elation.

"Tell me," Lu said.

"I've made the cheerleading squad. Josie and Martha helped me practice all summer. All three of us are in!"

Cheerleading squad. Had Frances told her she had signed up for it?

"That's great," Lu said. "I didn't know you were trying out."

"I didn't tell you? I guess I must have forgotten. But I wanted to share the news."

Cheerleading squad. Frances had mentioned something vaguely at dinner last week—something along the lines of, "It'd be fun to be a cheerleader." But they hadn't stayed on that subject—Frances never told her how much she was into it.

"It's great news," Lu said. "Do you know the other girls?"

"Most," Frances said, "and some of the boys—the ones I met at the pool club, anyway."

Lu's head whirled with the news.

"I'm really happy for you," she said.

"You know those dresses we saw the other day?"

Lu remembered. "With all the bows?"

Frances giggled. "Yeah! We can use them to decorate the pom-poms."

Lu laughed. "I'll try to snag them for you."

They paused. Lu almost heard Frances's smile through the line.

"Listen, I only have a minute. Martha's mom just showed up. She's taking us to the mall to celebrate. I'll e-mail later, okay?"

"Okay," Lu said.

Frances hung up. Lu placed the receiver back in its cradle. Frances wouldn't e-mail—not today, anyway. Lu knew that already.

She stared at the book on her desk. The thought of finding the play again in that oversized tome daunted her. Science, World History, Math, all were crammed into her backpack, waiting for her attention. Jack's music had only gotten louder to drown out the TV. She needed a break—a real break.

She slipped on a sweatshirt and headed downstairs. Mom and Ron were leaving.

"I'm taking a walk," she told them.

"Be back for dinner," Mom replied.

# 14 – Lu-Ellen Zimmer

### Into the woods

Lu decided to head into the woods behind their yard. There she'd find some quiet.

The forest belonged to a trucking company that had once operated a terminal in the northeast corner of its large property. Lu's street was the forest's southern boundary. During long summer days, Lu and Frances used to hike about twenty minutes into the property to reach a gentle stream. They'd spend hours exploring up and down its course. They always ended up at the same spot: an eddy that pooled at the foot of a large boulder. They called the place Frog Hollow. They invented long, complicated games where they were brave explorers dealing with unusual, sometimes magical creatures that all looked like frogs.

After so many summers of back-and-forth, they had trampled down a narrow path from her backyard to their secret playground. The path was still visible, if overgrown.

Lu lost her way twice, but this part of the forest had been her old stomping grounds, so she wasn't worried. When she finally reached the stream, she realized that she had veered off because she was at least a bend downstream from the Hollow. She followed the bank upstream, soothed by the bubbling water. When she heard the chirrup of a frog answered by another, she knew she was close. The boulder loomed behind the next tree.

As she rounded the tree, she stopped. Next to the boulder, crouched very still, pointing a camera right at the water's edge, was Blos Pease, his wiry orange hair catching reflections of sunlight through the trees.

Blos. Here. In Frog Hollow. The picture jarred.

She wanted to back up before he noticed her. But her foot caught a twig, and the wood snapped. Blos jerked his head up and around.

"Lu Zimmer."

He sounded frightened. He hadn't expected her, either.

"It's okay, Blos. You can go back to what you were doing. I'm just passing through."

"I'm taking photographs," Blos said.

"Yes, I know. Sorry I interrupted."

"I walked down the stream. You know it flows near our house before it heads up to the town line."

She did not know. She didn't really care. She took another step back.

"Ms. R said I should take pictures for the paper."

It crossed Lu's mind that pictures for the paper were supposed to be about school activities, not frogs in a stream. But she didn't correct him. She wanted to be by herself. She needed to shake him off.

"Go ahead. I'll leave you alone."

He didn't take the hint. He never took hints. He stood up and stepped toward her.

"I can show you what I've taken so far."

"Don't you want to print them first?"

"The camera is digital. It has a view screen."

She couldn't slow him down. He was right next to her, shoving the screen under her nose.

"I can replay them."

She felt trapped.

"Okay. Show me."

He did. A series of stills flashed on the small screen, shots filled with greens, yellows, rusts, and small patches of blue as they chronicled Blos's walk from his house through the woods along the stream. One was of Frog Hollow. The last one showed a circular ripple.

"I just missed him," Blos said. "I was waiting for him to come up so I could try again."

But Lu wasn't thinking about frogs.

"Can you back up the pictures? Like two or three?"

"Sure," Blos said.

He pressed a button. She saw a picture of the boulder, a picture of trees, a picture of a bend in the stream from afar, another picture of a bend in the stream from afar.

"Stop," she said. "Can I see that?"

"It is just a gap in the trees," Blos said.

"Yeah, but what's in that gap?"

Blos squinted. He pressed a few more buttons, and the picture zoomed in.

"That is a trailer," he said, "and some people working in a garden."

The trailer was on the other side of the stream, off the trucking property. And the garden looked huge. Lu wondered why she and Frances had never noticed it. The figures in the picture were indistinct.

"Where's this picture from?" she asked.

"I will show you," Blos said.

Before she had time to think, Blos started walking upstream. Lu ran to catch up.

"It was past that bend, over there," he said.

They passed the bend, and sure enough, a large gap opened on the other side of the stream. Lu stopped in the shade of a tree and held Blos back before he went any farther. When he turned to look at her, she covered her lips with a finger. She couldn't read his expression, but he reacted by crouching low, as if to hide from something.

"It's okay," she whispered. "Just, let's not be heard."

Across the stream was an enormous garden—more of a field, she thought—surrounded by tall bushes, the stream, and a fence that ended just at the gap in the woods. She had never seen so many plants rise so tall and thick, almost wild with their huge and varied leaves and fruits, yet lined up in civilized rows. It bore no resemblance to the neat vegetable patch Mom kept in a corner of their yard.

Perched above the garden was a weathered chicken coop and a trailer on cement blocks.

Lu immediately recognized Salman. He stood in the middle of the field, in a spot where plants had been cut down, scooping shovelfuls of black earth from a wheelbarrow. A large, blond-haired woman in even larger overalls walked away from him with another shovel in her hand.

"When you're done with the row, hon," the woman said, "you can call it a day."

Salman nodded but did not reply. He kept shoveling. The breeze shifted, and Lu smelled the pungent odor of manure.

Eew . . .

When the woman disappeared behind the trailer, Salman stopped shoveling and gazed across the stream.

Lu stood still, holding her breath. But Salman didn't see her or Blos: he was looking up, into the treetops. He grinned before he returned to his shoveling.

From above, a huge bird swooped down. And Lu had that fleeting sensation again, of alighting and folding her wings, as if she were the crow, landing at the edge of the field.

Salman glanced up at the trailer, then put the shovel down and reached into a pocket. He pulled out something shiny.

Lu watched the shiny thing, fascinated by the way it twinkled in the sunlight. She didn't move, yet she sensed wings stretch out, a hop, a flap, and the snap of a beak grabbing the metal object. She watched the bird fly up to the treetops and out of sight. When she looked down again, Salman had emptied the wheelbarrow and was raking the manure flat.

"Salman Page!" Blos yelled.

What was Blos doing? Hadn't she asked him to keep quiet? She wanted to yank Blos back.

Salman straightened. He shaded his eyes with a hand. Blos stepped out into the sunlight and waved. Salman's jaw dropped at first, then morphed into a smile. In a voice no louder than conversation, Salman answered, "Wait there. I won't be long."

Lu wanted to vanish. She'd been caught snooping.

Within a few minutes, Salman finished raking and returned the wheelbarrow, rake, and shovel behind the trailer. Lu heard the snap of a screen door opening and shutting, followed by a second snap a minute later.

Salman reappeared. He had changed his pants. He crossed the stream over a series of stones that jutted out from the water. His eyebrows were crinkled up in puzzlement.

"I told them I'm going for a walk," he said when he reached Blos. "How'd you get here?"

"Lu and I walked along the stream," Blos said.

"Lu?" Salman said.

Lu knew she needed to appear, right away. She should have stepped forward when Blos did. But instead she retreated farther into the shade. It was ridiculous, really. She had followed Blos into the woods and they had stumbled upon Salman's place. No harm in that. Yet she felt as though she had been spying on him. She was too embarrassed to be seen now.

Blos—who, of course, didn't get it—pointed at her. "She is back there."

Salman didn't seem angry.

"Let's go there, too," he said.

# 15—Salman Page

**Salman smiled. Lu smiled, too.**

Blos's appearance was exactly what he needed, Salman thought.

"I have been taking pictures," Blos said.

"For the paper?" Salman asked.

Blos nodded, obviously pleased about the correct guess. He was a breath of fresh air, Salman thought.

"Do you want to see them?" Blos asked.

They stood next to the tree where Lu had been hiding. She was obviously embarrassed at having been discovered. Salman wished that she wasn't. It was okay that she'd come. He was glad to see her. Glad to have an excuse to avoid the trailer.

Ozzy had been in a dark mood for days. He hardly

spoke, rooted in front of the TV, not showering nor shaving nor even changing his clothes, guzzling one beer after another. If this had been a cartoon, black clouds arcing lightning would have been roiling around him.

Tina worried.

"He's been low a long time," she said.

Salman feared an explosion. Ozzy had never hit him, but in the man's current state, Salman wasn't sure what he might do if Salman crossed him. He drank more and more, becoming less and less coherent. Tina had scheduled an appointment for him that afternoon at the outpatient clinic at the veterans' hospital.

Salman heard the pickup's engine roar. Lu jumped. Blos didn't seem to notice.

"It is a digital camera," Blos said. "I can show you every picture even before they are printed."

"That sounds cool," Salman said.

The thin layer of gravel crunched under the truck's wheels. Ozzy and Tina were gone. Salman breathed easier. Blos pointed to the screen and explained how each button worked.

"This is the picture of your garden. Lu wanted to see it."

Lu turned away, as if she was getting ready to run. A small part of Salman twinged inside.

"But I still need a few more good shots for tomorrow's meeting," Blos continued.

Blos meant the meeting Ms. R had called for the kids working on the paper. Salman had been invited, too.

"Hey, I can take a picture of the two of you. You know, a new student and his d.b."

Before either Salman or Lu had time to protest, Blos began snapping pictures of each of them.

"Wait," Lu said.

Blos stopped.

Lu sighed. "How about you just take one of us, together?"

Blos thought about it. "Okay."

Salman and Lu eyed each other, then stood at arm's length. Lu pushed her glasses up her nose. Salman ran his fingers through his hair.

"Ready?" Blos asked.

Salman smiled. Lu smiled, too.

"Great," Blos said. "Perfect. Do you want to see it?"

"No, thank you," Lu said.

Salman shook his head.

"I will print it," Blos said. "It will be even better."

Salman watched Lu. Her gaze was following the watercourse downstream.

"You're heading home?" he asked.

Salman's question had been meant for Lu, but Blos answered it.

"Yes. Then I can print it."

Blos tucked his camera into its case and slung it over his shoulder.

"I will show you the picture when it is printed," he said, "at the meeting, tomorrow."

"Okay, Blos. Bye," Salman said.

As Blos left them, Lu said, "Bye." She stepped in the opposite direction, following the stream's path. After a second's hesitation, Salman stepped with her.

"Was this the way you came?" he asked.

She nodded. They walked in silence.

They reached an eddy in the stream, with a large boulder at one end. Lu climbed the boulder and sat down. Salman wasn't sure what to do. He wanted to stay with her, but did she want him to? She might not appreciate his following her around.

"There's enough room," Lu said.

That small part of him inside fluttered.

The rock was craggy and poked at him through his jeans. But there was space for two on top. The brightness of the day had begun to fade, and the breeze felt cooler. Salman hugged his knees to keep warm. Lu hugged hers, too.

An uncomfortable silence settled between them. Salman turned his head to look at Lu, but she was looking away. She seemed so shy, or embarrassed, he wasn't sure which.

Then Bird flew down with a caw, startling them. He

landed next to the stream and eyed the water carefully. Lu shook her head.

"The frogs won't come out," she told the crow, "not if they can see you."

How did Lu know Bird was fishing for frogs?

"He might be after minnows," Salman said.

Lu shrugged, but Salman caught the hint of a smile.

To prove them both wrong, Bird flew up and perched himself on Salman's knees. Salman hoped the crow wouldn't rip his pants. Bird eyed Salman and Lu, each in turn.

Lu stretched out a hand and hesitated. Salman saw her face open with curiosity.

"Do you think he'd let me pet him?" she whispered.

"You can try," Salman said.

Slowly, steadily, Lu reached over. She touched Bird's chest. The crow half shut his eyes, as if with pleasure. The base of Salman's throat tingled. He swallowed.

"He's so big," Lu said.

Bird cocked his head, hopped off Salman's knees onto the boulder, and pecked at a shiny spot in one of the crags. Then, after one last look at them, he flew up into a tree branch and cawed a few more times.

"I think Bird likes you," Salman said.

"I like him, too."

She sounded breathless. Salman's mood soared.

The crow settled down onto the branch, his head sunk between his shoulders. The pose reminded Salman of the first time he'd seen Bird: Salman's second day at the Royals' trailer. Salman had just finished drying the breakfast dishes when Tina shooed him outside. She hadn't been mean, but she was firm.

"I like my coffee in peace. We'll work the garden when I'm done."

Not having had much by way of sleep, Salman felt too tired to explore. He walked down to the chicken coop, looking for a clear patch of grass to lie down in, when he came to the huge maple at the edge of the forest. One of its branches stuck straight out before curving up, like an arm beckoning. The branch was low and solid, and Salman climbed onto it without much difficulty. He leaned back into the trunk, where he fit into a smooth hollow, as if it had been made for him. He shut his eyes.

He must have dozed off because he never did hear the crow land. Tina's call jolted him awake.

"Salman Page. Where are you? I want you in the garden—now!"

The crow sat hunched in front of him. It opened one eye.

"Coming," Salman said, but not too loud.

Salman had always liked crows. They were smart. They were funny. And they always seemed to like him back.

The crow straightened and hopped sideways, away from Salman.

"Wait, bird, don't go," Salman whispered.

The crow cocked its head.

"I'm waiting!" Tina yelled.

Salman glanced toward the garden.

"Be right there," he said.

The crow hopped sideways again. But he didn't fly off, even when Salman scrambled down. At the foot of the tree, Salman whispered, "If you come back later, bird, I'll have something for you."

The crow seemed to nod before he flew off.

That morning Tina made Salman tie tomato plants to stakes. They used pieces of thin silver wire cut from a spool. As they finished with the last few plants, an old pickup pulled up in front of the trailer.

"That'll be Ozzy," Tina said.

She dusted her hands on her overalls.

"Do this last one, then come back to the trailer. I'll have some lunch ready."

Salman watched her walk back to the trailer. When she was out of sight, he leaned over and cut a length of wire to loop around the plant, then a second one that he slipped into a pocket.

Later that afternoon Tina had him lay hay around young vines.

"Those'll turn into pumpkins," she said. "Want 'em to grow big."

Ozzy brought the hay over in a wheelbarrow while Salman grabbed armfuls and tucked it around the plants. She let Salman quit by midafternoon.

"Come in later," she said. "You can help with dinner."

"There's more to do," growled Ozzy.

"We're out of hay," Tina said. "You need to pick up more."

Ozzy glared at Salman as if it was his fault and stomped away.

Salman returned to the maple tree. He was so tired, he almost didn't make it up to the branch. He nestled into the hollow, but even before he could shut his eyes, the crow landed in front of him with a rustling of feathers and a loud caw.

Salman smiled.

"Bird, you *are* eager."

The crow bobbed its head. Salman laughed. It wasn't much of a laugh, but it was Salman's first since he had left Mr. and Ms. D. It felt kind of nice.

The crow cocked his head once again. Salman fished into his pocket.

"I haven't forgotten," he said.

He leaned forward, the wire between his fingers, twisting it so that it twinkled in the sunlight. The crow jumped forward and nabbed it.

Salman grinned. The bird flew off. Salman cupped his hand over his forehead to watch the crow's flight.

"Come back again," he whispered.

And Bird had returned, every day, even on days when Salman had no more shiny things to offer, bringing him a snippet of happiness—like today, on this rock with Lu.

"Will Bird spend the night here?" Lu asked.

"I don't think so," Salman said. "He usually perches near the trailer."

"That's where you live," Lu said.

"For now."

Lu rested the side of her head on her knees, letting her glasses slide down.

"Why 'for now'?"

"It's a foster home. A temporary placement."

"You're going to move?"

Salman shrugged.

"Sometime."

"Are your foster parents okay?"

"As long as I do my chores."

Salman wasn't sure how much he wanted to reveal. After all, he wasn't entirely certain Lu wanted him there with her. But she had started talking—and asking some pretty personal questions.

"Why were you hiding before?" he said.

Lu didn't answer right away. Her grip on her knees tightened and she squinted down at the stream.

"I'm not sure," she said. "When Blos showed me the picture, I was curious about the garden, and before I could stop him, we were there. And then I saw you, and well, it was like we were spying or something. . . ."

"And you thought I'd be pissed off."

Lu nodded.

Salman put a hand on hers, just long enough to feel

her warmth before he pulled his away. A thrill went up his arm.

"I'm *glad* you came," he said.

He meant it. Lu looked up at him. Her eyes were shiny. She seemed so relieved.

"Thanks," she said.

She took a deep breath and jumped down from the boulder.

"I'd better head home," she said. "I have a huge amount of homework waiting."

"Can I walk with you?"

"Sure!"

She led them down a barely visible path away from the stream. Salman was uncertain about where they were headed, but Lu didn't hesitate. They passed under branches, around stumps.

"You know your way around," Salman said.

"I used to walk here all the time," Lu replied.

"I've never spent much time in woods."

Lu stopped at a tree that had fallen over and was blocking the path.

"I guess you must know Bridgeport better."

Salman stood next to her.

"Not really. I left when I was five."

What was safe to tell her? When he was a few hours old, he had been wrapped in a bloody sheet and left next to a Dumpster near a Bridgeport hospital. A sanitation worker had found him, blue from exposure. Salman had spent months in a hospital, five years with the kindest woman in the world, then years shipped from one foster home to the next.

"I don't have any family," he said.

Lu didn't seem to believe him.

"No family? At all?"

"Nope."

He turned away and climbed over the tree trunk. He didn't want to talk about this.

He was a foundling. No one had ever wanted him. Except maybe for Emolia Brown, his first foster mother. But she was private.

Lu followed him over the log and led him farther down the woods. He heard a rustle overhead: Bird was following them, too. In another ten minutes, they reached an opening, and Salman saw the rear of Lu's house across a long yard.

Lu stopped.

"You know," she said, "I came here to be alone."

Something sank inside Salman. "Sorry—"

"No, no," she interrupted. "What I'm trying to say is that I'm really glad I wasn't."

All of a sudden, Salman's heart began to sing. He grinned.

"I'm glad I wasn't, also."

This time Lu smiled.

# 16—Blos Pease

### Picture after picture

Blos connected the camera to the computer. He clicked on the photo program. "Save to C drive?" Yes. The computer whirred. One thumbnail appeared. Then another. Picture after picture formed on his screen. His house. His path. The trees. The stream. The garden. The boulder. The pool. Salman. Lu. Both of them.

"Download complete."

Blos disconnected the camera. Folded the wire into a box. Stored the camera in its case. Placed the case on the shelf—on the back of the shelf.

"You don't want to drop it," his mother had said.

No. He would keep it safe.

He returned to the computer. A window had appeared.

"View pictures?"

He clicked "Yes."

The first photo came up.

The picture of Mom was okay. No red eye. The one of the house was pretty good, too. He had taken it from the street. A street he had lived on all his life. A street that was safe. A dead end.

"There's no through traffic," his mother had said.

When he was nine she taught him to ride a bicycle up and down their street.

"Helmet first," she said. "Stay on the right side. Watch for people and cars."

That was hard, watching for people and cars, and keeping his balance, and pedaling forward, and staying on the right side. For weeks she coaxed him, running beside him. Then one Sunday, she brought him to the parking lot behind Springfalls Elementary School. No one was there.

"Just stay on the bike and pedal," she said.

He did. He pedaled and pedaled. He rode onto the grass and fell down. That hurt. But he laughed because he had kept his balance the whole way.

Mom laughed, too.

He got back on and pedaled some more.

For a month Mom brought him there every Sunday, and he was able to do it! He kept his balance. He pedaled forward. Mom asked him to go along the edges, make circles in the middle, cross back and forth. And he did it. Over and over.

"Ready to try it on our street?" she asked.

Blos nodded. He was ready. He pedaled up and down their street. He watched for people and cars. He was safe.

The next photo was the path.

It started at the bottom of the cul-de-sac, behind the tiny neighborhood playground where he had played every day when he was little. That's how he had discovered the path.

"We can walk there, if you want," his mom had said.

But Blos was scared. The trees were big. The bushes were prickly. And there was a stream. He might get wet. When he was four or five, he took his mother's hand and followed her a few steps into the woods. She pointed out flowers. She picked up pebbles. Blos held on tight. They turned back around.

At five he started school. During recess he went down the slide in the school playground, over and over. Sometimes kids came up to him and said strange things. Mean things. Every afternoon, when it wasn't raining, he went back to the little playground at the end of the street. He was safe there. The neighbors knew him. They left him alone. But by fourth grade the swings began getting too small. The slide, too short. And the path did not look so scary anymore.

He placed pebbles in the stream. He watched the ripples move around the stones in wonderful strange patterns. He placed piles of stones in circles. In squares. In triangles.

In fifth grade he went down the path to the bend, just far enough so that he could still see the opening to the playground, but deep enough so he could not hear the kids playing there. He built little dams across the stream with fallen sticks and rocks. In sixth grade he set out to build a bridge. A little bridge over a shallow spot—just strong enough to hold him up. Every afternoon after school, when it was not too cold or wet, he tied branches together with string. He lined them up. One next to the other. Like a board. He got more string and tied those together. And then he made a pile of rocks on the stream's edge. A neat pile. Flat at the center. And a second pile across the stream. It took him two weeks. When he laid the plank of branches across—he had a bridge!

He was so proud! He told Mom. He had her come and see it. Saturday morning.

But when they got there, the plank was broken. The piles of rocks had been pushed down.

"Oh, Blos!" Mom said.

Blos cried. He cried and cried.

He did not build another bridge. But he did go deeper along the path. Away from the playground. Away from the people who broke his bridge.

The next photo showed trees. Then the stream. Then the garden.

The garden had a lot of plants. Not like the flower bed in front of their house. Mom kept that neat and small and organized. Blos watered it every day in the summer. He took out the can. The one with the big spout and lots of little holes. He filled it with the hose. He sprinkled the water over each plant, like a rain shower, one at a time, until the can was empty. Then he refilled the can and sprinkled some more.

You could not do that in Salman's garden.

The boulder. The pool. Salman.

Salman. Lu was Salman's d.b. Did d.b.s visit their assigned students in their gardens? Elaine Egger, his d.b., never visited him in his garden. No one did. Ever.

Lu.

And there was the crow. On a branch. Just above her. Was that Salman's crow? He was not sure. Crows all looked the same to him.

Lu and Salman.

And the crow. Yes, he was pretty sure that was the same crow.

The picture was good. He had gotten both Lu and Salman clearly. From head to toe. And the tree framed them.

Mom had told him about framing when she gave him his first camera.

"The lens is like a box. You only get to see what's inside the box. You want to make sure that what you want to see is where you want it in the box."

He liked putting things in a box. You took a messy landscape, with no beginning and no edges, and you decided: this part I am going to keep. You put it in a box. He was good at putting things in boxes.

He learned that sometimes framing happened inside the picture. Objects made edges, just like a box, and you could photograph them so that the edges made it look like a box within a box.

The tree made a line between Salman and Lu, and the branches above, another one. The crow sat on one of the branches, in its own box.

Blos liked it. Three boxes in one picture.

He took the photo paper from the drawer. Mom called from the kitchen. "Found a good photo?"

"Yes. I did."

"Can I see it?"

"Okay."

This was a very good photo. For the school paper. He would bring it in to show Ms. R. And Salman. And Lu.

# 17 – Salman Page

### Lost

As Salman walked through the woods, he replayed his conversation with Lu over and over. She had been embarrassed to be caught spying but was glad to be with him. When she had smiled saying goodbye, her whole body had smiled—from her pretty eyes behind her glasses to her long, graceful fingers. She had been happy that she was going to see him tomorrow.

What a strange sensation, Salman thought, that he was happy because Lu wanted to be with him.

He stopped. He had been walking for a while. Lu had told him to look for the stream.

"It'll lead you back to the trailer," she had said.

Why hadn't he reached it? He had lost the path early

on, but he thought he had headed in the right direction. He looked ahead, to either side, and off to his right he saw a large boulder. That was where he needed to go. But when he reached the boulder, he didn't see the stream. Instead, the land rose. The forest floor became rockier. Perhaps if he climbed higher, he'd catch a view of the stream. He plodded ahead. Still no stream.

As the late-afternoon light began to fade, the woods became quieter. A bird whistled. A squirrel chattered. And then Salman heard *whirs* and *thu-wunks*, faintly, and then more constant and sometimes overlapping, getting louder as he climbed higher. The sounds were familiar, but he couldn't place them.

He went through a row of trees to overgrown bushes and weeds. The sky opened up. Light flowed in. The sounds became more distinct. He pushed through the tall grasses and stepped onto crumbling pavement. A boy on a skateboard headed straight for him.

"Hey!"

The skateboarder maneuvered to one side, avoiding Salman but unbalancing himself in the process. The skateboard skidded off, and the boy landed on his butt.

"What the hell do you think you're doing?" the boy said.

Three other boys came running.

"Rob, what happened?"

Rob Puckett dusted himself off.

"This jerk came out of the bushes, just as—"

"It's Crow!" a beefy boy said.

Salman recognized them. All but the smallest were from the junior high school. The beefy one, almost Salman's height, was called Sean. Most kids were afraid of him. But Sean listened to Rob Puckett, who was now approaching Salman with hard eyes and a mean smile.

"Crow," he said. "Need to be careful where you land."

The smallest kid, no older than nine or ten—a mini Rob—tugged at Rob's sleeve.

"Are you going to hit him?"

Rob pulled his arm away and glowered. The kid backed off.

"Naw," Rob said. "I want to see how well he flies."

The tallest boy of the bunch, a few inches taller than Salman, shuffled.

"Rob, he hasn't done nothing—"

"Shut up, Walt."

Without taking his eyes off Salman, Rob addressed all three boys.

"Someone lend Crow your board."

The little kid stepped forward.

"Want to use mine?"

"Okay, Jimmy," Rob said.

He took Jimmy's skateboard and jammed it into Salman's arms.

"Ever ride?" Rob said.

Salman shook his head. Rob smiled.

"Good."

The boys marched Salman down the parking lot to where they had set up makeshift ramps and obstacles using plywood boards and bricks.

"Walt, show him how to ride," Rob said.

The tall, curly-haired boy put his skateboard down and showed Salman how to push and the rudiments of maneuvering.

"You lean this way to turn," Walt said.

Salman tried. It wasn't so hard. He had a good sense of balance, and the skateboard was fairly stable. He tried a couple of turns and managed them well enough. He followed Walt around the perimeter of the obstacle course, then stepped on the back lip to push the front of the skateboard up. He jumped off, just as Walt had. Salman caught the skateboard with his hand.

Rob scowled. "You sure you've never done this before?"

"Never," Salman said.

Rob's expression was clear: he didn't believe him.

Salman knew he had a gift—being coordinated and graceful. Everyone commented on it, every place he stayed. Even Tina told Ozzy, "Only show him somethin' once, and he gets it. Like he can read the motions."

But he wasn't about to explain that to Rob Puckett.

"Follow me," Rob said.

He set off around the ramps and piles of bricks. Salman hesitated. The beefy boy, Sean, moved closer.

Salman was taller, but Sean was heavier and looked as if he had practice hitting people.

Salman stepped onto Jimmy's board and pushed off in Rob's direction.

They circled the obstacle course twice before Rob veered in. Salman followed. Rob snaked in and out of a line of little brick pyramids. Slower, Salman followed. Rob waited. When Salman rounded the last pyramid, Rob hopped back onto his board and aimed for one of the ramps.

"This way!" he yelled.

Rob picked up speed, crouched low, then *swomp,* he flew off the end and landed back on his board.

Salman stopped. He couldn't do that. He knew he couldn't. He had neither the speed nor the practice. Rob circled around.

"C'mon, Crow. Let's see you fly."

Salman shook his head.

"You're too chicken," Rob said.

"I can't do it," Salman said.

"He's chicken!" Rob yelled. He stopped, inches from Salman. "He isn't a crow. He's a skinny black chicken!"

Rob began making clucking noises. Soon the other boys were, too. They surrounded Salman, clucking and laughing.

"Chic-ken!" "Cluck, cluck, cluck." "Pwah! Pwah!"

Jimmy, the littlest, grabbed his board back.

"Don't want chicken mess on this!"

The others laughed.

"Get out of here, Chicken," Rob said. He pushed Salman hard, and Salman fell over. The boys' laughter redoubled.

"Maybe he wants to lay an egg," the beefy one said.

"You've got it, Sean," Rob said. "But he'll need to lose his pants first."

Sean glanced at Rob, and the two began converging on Salman.

Salman scrambled. He saw an opening next to Walt and dove through. He ran as fast as he could, straight for the nearest bushes.

"He's getting away," Jimmy said.

Salman heard the *thunk* of several skateboards hitting the pavement. He didn't look back. He kept on running.

"Let him go," Rob said. "Chicken's going home to roost."

# 18 – Puck

### Make him stumble

"Tell me more about my namesake's mate," my queen commanded.

"He is an angry man," I replied. "He is jealous of the foster mother's affection for the boy."

The crow had perceived an imbalance in the man but could not explain it.

"Does he put the boy in danger?"

"I am not sure, milady. Your namesake is a strong woman. But I fear that should the man come to rage, he may be stronger."

My queen frowned. "I want the boy safe."

She stood very still. I waited, as I knew I must.

"Remove the man," she said at last.

I blanched. I could feel it.

"How, milady?"

"Make him stumble. Addle his mind. Follow him, Puck, and pounce at the first opportunity."

And so I was ordered to interfere. Again. First with one. Then with the other.

"I expect alacrity, Puck."

I bowed. "I do as you command."

She folded her hands before her.

"And when you are done, you may report to the king."

I froze, head bowed.

"I am no fool, Puck. Let him know that though he commands you, I commanded you first."

I did not see her leave. But the smell of her brimstone lingered.

Ah, Puck. What was I to do? The queen's anger festered. And once again, I was stuck in the middle.

# 19 – Salman Page

### Bruised, scratched, muddied

The last Salman heard of the boys was their laughter as he crashed through the tall weeds and scraped himself against branches. He ran hard, past trees, around boulders, down a hill. He had no idea where he was, but he kept running, over dead tree trunks, past hanging vines. He ran until he tripped and fell forward on some rocks. He had knocked all the wind out of himself and he gasped for air, unable to sit up.

His breath came ragged and painful. Every intake brought the smell of rotting leaves and earth. Carefully, he pushed himself up and touched the side of his face. His fingers came away wet and red—he must have cut himself. A high whistle startled him.

Salman saw no one. Twilight had set in. Woods surrounded him. He was bruised, scratched, muddied, and his shirt was torn at the sleeve. Tina was going to be furious.

That was, if he ever saw her again.

A loud rustle descended from the branches above him. Salman jumped to the side. A pain shot up from his ankle where it had hit a rock.

"Caw!"

Bird landed on a stone a few feet away from him. Someone he knew! Salman had never been so happy to see his friend.

"Bird!"

The crow hopped a few feet farther away.

"Caw!"

"I'm lost," Salman said. "Don't run away."

Bird hopped farther.

"Caw!"

Why was Bird behaving this way?

"Where are you going?"

Bird flapped his wings and hopped farther still, cawing yet again.

"You want me to follow?"

"Caw!"

Salman could have sworn that the bird nodded. He followed. In the dim light, and with a painful foot, he hobbled toward Bird. As soon as he came within a yard or two, the crow flapped his wings again and hopped away. Salman followed. The forest grew darker, but Salman never lost the black form with the shiny eyes.

"Caw!"

Bird flew ahead, up onto a hulking shape. As Salman walked toward the crow, he heard the gurgle of water. His foot splashed into the stream. Bird was perched atop the boulder that Salman and Lu had sat upon not so long ago. Relief swept over Salman so quickly, he almost cried.

"I'm near the trailer."

Bird flew down next to Salman. The boy crouched, and just as Lu had earlier that day, he stroked Bird's chest. The crow let him, half shutting his eyes.

"Thank you," Salman said. "I know where to go from here."

Bird bobbed his head once and flew off.

There was precious little light. Salman had to hurry now. He kept to the stream, which was easy to see and hear even as night fell in earnest. The moon shone a crescent. When he found the gap to the Royals' garden, he waded across the stream, not worrying whether he wet his sneakers.

He stopped for a second to wash his face. Maybe he'd get past Tina before she noticed the mess he was in.

But the trailer was dark when he reached it. The TV was off. Salman opened the door.

"Tina?"

No one answered. This was creepy. He groped for the light switch.

"Ozzy?"

He flipped the switch. The lights came on. Smelly beer cans littered the coffee table. No one was there— no one but Salman. The trailer seemed to grow all of a sudden.

He wasn't sure what to do. Then he caught a glimpse of himself in a mirror and decided to take a shower. Once clean, he dug some food out of the refrigerator, ate a late dinner, and tidied up the mess Ozzy had left behind.

Still, no one showed up.

He didn't turn on the TV. The silence came as a relief after the nonstop noise they had been living in these last weeks. He completed his homework and went to bed early, puzzling where Tina and Ozzy might have gone.

The next morning, he woke up stiff and sore. His ankle had swelled, but he could walk on it. Ozzy and Tina had not returned. As he made his own breakfast, he started to worry. He didn't like his foster home, but it was the only place he had. What was he supposed to do if they didn't show up?

He opened the top drawer of his dresser. Under his socks, he kept the papers his social worker had given him, including her number if he needed to call—long-distance, he realized. The Royals were probably just visiting somewhere. They'd be back. And if he phoned his social worker, the number'd show up on the Royals' bill and he'd have to explain to Ozzy why he'd called.

He shut the drawer. If no one was home this afternoon when he got back from school, he'd phone then. Right now, he had a meeting to get to.

The thought gave him energy. Lu would be there.

# 20 – Lu-Ellen Zimmer

### The school paper

Mom was tired last night and didn't eat much of her dinner. Dad had insisted on serving the meal.

"You need rest, Marianne."

Everyone had pitched in. Even usually oblivious Ricky had helped clean up. Mom went to bed early.

In the morning, Mom had more energy, but Lu noted that Dad was fixing breakfast.

"I'll eat a banana," Lu said. "I have an early meeting."

Ricky looked up from his bowl of cereal. "With your boy-oy-friend?"

"Mom!"

"That's enough, Ricky."

Much to Lu's annoyance, Ron and Jack were grinning.

"I have a meeting for the school paper," Lu said, "if you *have* to know."

"You were picked," Jack said. "That's pretty cool."

Jack was okay, sometimes. Lu unhooked a banana from the bunch on the counter and peeled it. She watched Dad wash dishes, then dry his hands on a towel. He eyed the banana.

"That's all you're having?" he said.

"The meeting's in ten minutes," she said.

"I'll drive you," Dad said. "You'll be there in five."

"I want a ride," said Ricky.

"The bus will take you," Mom said.

"There's a piece of toast," Dad told Lu.

Lu sighed. She took the toast. Just 'cause Mom ate like a horse, why did she have to?

She sulked during the short ride to school.

"You know, Lu . . . ," Dad said.

"I know, I know. You're only doing what's best."

That's what he always said when he ordered them around—like making her eat the stupid toast. Dad grinned.

"Well, yes. But that wasn't what I was going to say."

They had arrived, and Lu put her hand on the door handle, ready to jump out.

"Your mom needs your help," Dad said. "Now especially."

Lu nodded. She knew that.

"Try not to fight with Ricky too much. Okay?"

She huffed. *He's* the one who always started it.

"Why don't you tell *him*?"

Dad lowered his chin and stared at her over his glasses. "I will."

Lu felt an annoying blush wash over her cheeks. "Okay."

She remembered to say "bye" before shutting the car door. Dad meant well, she knew, but sometimes he was just clueless. Ricky never listened.

The meeting took place in the school paper's office— not that it was much of an office. Two computers, a printer, two tables, and a bunch of chairs were jammed together in a small, windowless room. It must have once been a storage closet of some kind. A dozen kids perched themselves on available surfaces. Ms. R stood by one of the computers.

"Thank you for coming," she began.

She went over the rules for computer use, timetables, what could and couldn't be printed. Lu watched the other kids. Blos stood in the front. He had arrived early, she was sure. He was busy taking notes. Most of the other kids were either nodding at what Ms. R was saying or beginning to space. Lu tried to catch Ruthie's attention, but she wasn't looking in Lu's direction. Salman arrived a few minutes late.

"Ah, Salman," Ms. R said. "I'm glad you came."

Salman nodded. What had happened to him? Lu wondered. He was limping and a nasty lump rose out from one side of his face. He looked down when Lu raised an eyebrow.

"Future meetings will be in my homeroom," Ms. R said. "That way we'll be able to spread out."

She handed them forms to fill in and a schedule. She also gave assignments.

"I'd like each of you to write one short column by our next meeting," she said.

"I have some pictures," Blos said.

"Thank you, Blos. You've just reminded me. This year, we are in luck. We have our very own staff photographer."

"Do you want to see them?" Blos said.

"Certainly," said Ms. R, "once we're done with the meeting."

"One shows a new student and his d.b."

You had to admire Ms. R's patience.

"That sounds like an excellent topic. Who will team up with Blos to write the copy?"

No one volunteered. Lu felt sorry for Blos. She raised her hand.

"I'll try."

Ms. R brightened.

"Thank you, Lu. I'll see you all next week in my classroom."

Students jammed the door as they exited. Blos headed straight for Ms. R.

"I took it last night," he said. "It is pretty good."

Ms. R craned her neck.

"This is a very nice picture. But you'll have to get the permission of the people in it before we can print it."

"Okay," said Blos.

Blos turned to Lu.

"Will you give permission?"

She took the print from Blos's hands. Lu and Salman stood in front of a large tree, wearing put-on smiles. Blos must have been farther back than she remembered because he had also captured a great deal of the trunk and some of the lower branches. On the very lowest branch, almost exactly between them, Bird sat preening his feathers. For some reason, Bird's presence didn't surprise her. Salman and Bird belonged together. And Salman . . . Well, he looked almost regal in his bedraggled clothes. He stood straight, a head taller than her, and his eyes were particularly large, or hers were particularly small behind her glasses. The contrast was startling.

Did she want the photo in the paper? Everyone knew she was Salman's d.b., but she wasn't sure she wanted to advertise it.

Almost all the students had left the office by now. Blos kept glancing at his watch while panic crept across his face.

"Homeroom is in three minutes," he said.

She handed the photo back to him.

"I'm not sure," she said. "Let's talk to Salman."

Blos nodded and ran off, almost knocking Ms. R over in the doorway.

"That boy's always in a hurry," Ms. R said.

When they were both gone, Lu approached Salman.

"Blos wants to print a photo of us."

"I think you suggested it," he said.

She stared at Salman for a few seconds. "I forgot!" It *had* been her idea. She had told him to take a picture of the two of them, together.

"What happened to you?" she asked.

Salman touched the edge of the bump with the tips of his fingers. The bruise made his dark skin even darker.

"I ran into Rob Puckett and some of his friends," he said.

"This morning?"

"No. Last night."

"Does it hurt?"

Salman smiled. "Not too much."

She reached up with the tips of her fingers and sensed the heat of his face without even touching it. She wished that she could make the hurt go away with a touch or a kiss, the way her mother did when she was little. She let her hand drop.

"Lu . . . ," he said.

The bell interrupted him. He stared at her. He didn't continue. She saw that he couldn't. That was okay. He had said enough.

"We'll talk at lunch?" Lu said.

Salman nodded, relief in his eyes.

"That sounds good."

She smiled.

She remembered the warmth in his voice all that morning.

# 21—Salman Page

**Without him with someone else**

Salman seated himself in Ms. R's classroom before he stashed the forms he still carried from the meeting into his pack. Ms. R had said they were supposed to be signed by a parent or guardian. He wondered if anyone was going to be around to sign his.

He found his Language Arts notes, printed today's date, and copied down their newest writing homework: "Describe a place you know well, and whether this place is important to you and why." Ms. R always gave strange assignments.

At lunch, the line moved slower than usual. Lu had already started eating by the time Salman made it to his seat across from her. Blos sat next to her, stiff with his bag unopened on the table, watching Salman the way a cat watched a bug before pouncing on it. Blos pulled a photo from under his bag.

"Ms. R says I need your permission to print it. Will you give it to me?"

Salman took the photo from Blos's hands. He noticed how shy Lu appeared in it, with her put-on smile. Her light brown hair shone, reflecting the shine of Bird's feathers. He almost laughed at the expression in her eyes that said, "Let's get this over with quick, please."

"Okay with you?" Salman asked Lu.

She shrugged and nodded at the same time. He slid the photo back to Blos.

"You have my permission, but I'll have to get Bird's first before you put his picture in the paper."

Blos exhaled. "Okay." He then emptied the contents of his sack, lined them up, and devoured them. He was set to run.

"I'll need a copy to show Bird," Salman said.

Blos paused.

"Take this one. I will print another one."

Lu waited until Blos had left before asking, "How are you going to get Bird's permission?"

"I'll ask."

She thoroughly chewed a bite of her sandwich before nodding.

Salman allowed himself to relax. He could be himself here.

The rest of the afternoon passed slowly. No one bothered him today. But his ankle continued to hurt whenever he walked on it too long, and he was grateful for the bus ride home.

His heart sank when he saw Ozzy's old pickup in front of the trailer. Although the Royals' absence had worried him, he had also enjoyed the respite from Ozzy's vigilance and Tina's chores. Besides, he was in no shape to work the garden.

But when he entered the trailer, he realized no work was planned for today.

Tina was sitting alone at the table, a glass of water, half drunk, in front of her. Her light hair flew every which way. Her shirt was wrinkled and stained. And when she lifted her head from her arms to look at Salman, he saw dark rings circling her bloodshot eyes.

"I'm going to crash," she said. "We'll talk later."

Ozzy wasn't there. As far as Salman could tell, he and Tina were alone on the property. Now, more than ever, Salman wanted to know what had happened.

As the afternoon slipped into evening, Salman grew hungry. He fixed a pot of rice on the stove, and a second pot to heat stewed tomatoes he'd found in the fridge. He was breaking a couple of eggs into a bowl when Tina ambled in from her bedroom, still wearing the same clothes, her eyes bleary but not as red. She took Salman's slim hand in her large ones.

"Don't you worry. The surgery went well."

"Surgery?"

Salman wasn't sure whom Tina was talking about. Did she mean Ozzy?

"He broke his leg—two places. They had to put a metal pin in."

Ozzy broke his leg? How? When? Tina walked over to the stove, lifted a pot cover, sniffed, and stirred.

"The tomatoes are bubbling," she said.

"The rice'll need five more minutes."

"Very good."

Salman felt crazy. He still had no idea where Ozzy was, Tina looked a total mess, and here they were, discussing dinner.

"What happened?" he asked.

Tina replaced the pot cover.

"He drank too much yesterday."

Ozzy drank too much every day, but Salman knew better than to say so.

"We had an appointment at the clinic. But when we got there . . ."

She paused and wiped a tear with the back of her hand.

"He stepped out of the truck and stumbled."

Salman glanced out the window at the truck as if it could confirm what had happened yesterday.

"He tried to catch himself, and twisted . . ."

She wiped her eyes again with her other hand.

"He screamed and screamed. The attendant called

the ER. And they had to take X-rays. And they wouldn't operate until he was soberer."

If they had operated on Ozzy and they had placed a pin in his leg, that meant he wasn't going to be coming home right away.

"How long is he going to be there?"

"A few days," Tina said. "They want to be sure there's no infection. And they want to start him on rehab."

Tina set the table. She laid out three settings. Salman watched her befuddlement as she stared at the extra setting and then put it back.

"Never been without him with someone else," she said.

They ate in silence. Tina cleaned up, shooing Salman away when he tried to help.

"Do your homework or something," she said.

Salman headed to his tiny room. He shut the door, grabbed his backpack from under the bed, and fished out the binder. He had the weekend to complete his homework, but there was nothing else to do—he didn't dare turn on the TV while Tina was in the main room. She had made it clear that she wanted to be alone.

Salman reread Ms. R's essay question. He had to think it through before he wrote—he didn't have room for rewrites. Ozzy'd be back in a few days—once they started his rehabilitation.

Salman printed his name, the date, the class, and thought some more.

# 22

## My bedroom is paneled with dark wood

Salman Page
October _____
Language Arts

TOPIC: Describe a place you know well, and
whether it is important to you and why.

    My bedroom is paneled with dark wood.
The window, small, comes more than halfway up
the narrow wall. It opens only a little, by sliding
a panel sideways. Through it I can see treetops
and the sky. Tonight I see the moon, cut down
to the thinnest sliver.

My bed is narrow. But the sheets are clean and the comforter warm. The pillow is a little lumpy—but I don't mind. My bed serves as the place where I sleep at night, the desk I work upon, and a storage cubicle for my shoes and pack underneath.

Against the opposite wall is my dresser. It has three drawers. It's made of wood, a shade lighter than the paneling. The finish is scratched, and two of the six handles are missing. But the drawers pull open smoothly, and in them I keep everything else I possess. The dresser isn't very full.

On top of the dresser is a lamp. I like the lamp. It is small, about the length of my forearm if you laid it sideways. It has a plain, white shade. But someone worked hard putting the base together: with clear plastic and a silver metal, he (or she) made it look like part of a chandelier. Stacked over an imitation-marble base are large, crystal-shaped pieces separated by decorated metal rings. When the bulb shines down on the pieces, they reflect pink and green sparkles.

The lamp isn't mine, nor is the bed, nor is the dresser. But the space within the room, when I shut the door and turn on the lamp, is private. The air I breathe, coming through the window, is mine. The quiet I hear is mine. The moments of solitude are mine. And so, although the furniture and walls and floor and door do not belong to me, my bedroom is important because within it, I keep me.

# 23–Puck

### No sympathy

"So? Have you sown discord, Puck?"

I nodded. I had tried to avoid this audience. But King Oberon had sent a messenger, and I could not refuse.

"She is a target of bullies, milord."

And so was the boy. But I did not tell milord. I had not told the queen, either, fear holding me silent.

"Excellent! And how does her relationship go with the boy?"

I was bound by the truth. "They are closer."

"Ah."

He was disappointed. The crow, on the other hand, had been thrilled. He thought the girl a noble creature.

And his pleasure about their friendship should have given me some.

"Tell me more about the girl, Puck."

I was careful with my words.

"She lives with her mother and father."

He nodded. "Any siblings?"

"Yes, milord. Three brothers, and her mother is with child."

"Really?"

I wanted to eat those words. His interest was too keen.

"Do not grow pale, Puck. How goes the brooding?"

No. No. No.

"The mother tires."

"And the babe?"

No!

I did not respond. Oberon leaned forward.

"I asked you a question, Puck."

"The babe is healthy."

He was thinking. Thinking about the innocent babe in the womb. His thoughts would only bring ill. I had to distract him.

"Your Majesty, I have news from milady."

"Queen Titania?"

"She knows that I report to you."

He narrowed his eyes.

"And does she know you are betraying her?"

My voice almost caught in fear.

"I have not betrayed her."

"She might not see your meddling that way, Puck."

I had acted under his orders! *He* had meddled. Forced me to interfere. But this did not matter. Not to the king.

"And what, Puck, have you told her about me?"

His words were very quiet. Too quiet.

"Naught, Your Majesty."

He nodded and stood.

"Very well. Then I order you, Puck, to tell the queen that if she does not leave this boy alone, I shall destroy what she holds most dear."

'Twas the crow's fault. A friend of my friend was also my friend. I had a duty to this boy. Oberon's injustice overwhelmed me. And then I became foolish, a foolish Puck.

"The boy is innocent, milord. He has never asked for her attention."

"But the queen showers it upon him. He must enjoy the boon her attentions provide. . . ."

I shook my head. "He does not know she exists."

"Then why?"

He clenched his fist. I was bound to answer, but I vowed silence. Any truthful answer would mean my end either by the king for its truth, or by the queen for my betrayal.

He took a step closer, and I wished to flee. But I could not. I had not been dismissed.

"Puck," he said, his voice sharp, "the queen has no particular sympathy for this boy, does she?"

I shook my head. A truth that was not a betrayal. She had never told Oberon that she had sympathy. She only provided attention. Attention that drove Oberon to rage.

"He's a tool," Oberon said.

He looked at me.

"I shall not ask for confirmation, Puck."

He turned, and in a flat voice he dismissed me. I fled in misery. My king and queen were at war, and I was torn between them.

# 24 – Lu-Ellen Zimmer

### It makes the coolest graphs

Lu was lonely. Lonelier than she'd felt since Frances had moved more than four months ago.

Something had changed, and she couldn't figure out what or why. Other than at lunch when she ate with Salman and Blos, no one at school talked to her anymore. Even Ruthie seemed to be avoiding her. And now Lu had become the butt of jokes.

"Hey, Bird Tamer," Bethany said that afternoon, "you've gone and caught a loon."

"Caught him a while back," Rob said. "Now she's writing stories for him."

Ruthie blushed. She must have told them that Lu had volunteered to write the copy for Blos's photo.

"Your crow's turned chicken, though," Sean said.

"She hasn't been giving him the right kind of feed," Rob said.

Kids laughed. Lu was relieved when Math started.

And home wasn't much better.

She tried, really tried, to be patient with Ricky. But he just wouldn't let up.

"Jimmy says you hang out with jerks," Ricky said.

"Jimmy is clueless," she said.

"His brother says your friends are dummies, and you're becoming one, too."

"That's enough, Ricky," Mom said. "Don't talk about people that way."

Dad, who had come home early, was at the counter making one of his power shakes for Mom. He gave Ricky a dark look. That didn't stop him.

"But her friends *are* weird," Ricky said. "You saw that Salman guy. Jimmy says he's a loser."

Ron walked in, ready to be driven to fencing practice. Ricky tried to enlist him.

"You remember Blos Pease?" Ricky said.

Ron thought for a moment.

"Nope."

"You know: wild orange hair, total weirdo."

"Oh yeah," Ron said. "What about him?"

"He's Lu's *friend*!"

"So?"

"He's *weird*."

"Let's go," Dad said. "We don't want to be late."

Ron grabbed his helmet and began following Dad out the door. He stopped at the threshold.

"You know, Lu," Ron said, "hanging with weird people can be tough."

"Thanks," Lu said.

Right—thanks. As if Ron were telling her something new.

When Dad returned, he organized dinner and made Mom lie down.

"You're not as young as you used to be," he told her.

At the table, Ricky started up again.

"Does Salman really caw like a crow?"

"That's enough!" Dad shouted.

Everyone tiptoed around after that. Dad almost never blew up. He really must have been concerned about something. Mom went to bed soon after.

When Lu tried to sleep that night, she tossed and turned. She felt exhausted, yet her mind raced. School sucked. Ricky was a total pain. And what was wrong with Mom?

Lu needed to calm herself somehow, so she decided to try a trick she had once overheard Dad tell Ron. She imagined the letter *A*, huge and bold, jet-black. Then she imagined it shifting from black to gray to white, then slowly fading until it disappeared entirely. Now the letter *B*. As *C* moved from black to dark gray, it sprouted wings. She noticed its eyes and beak—the eyes were friendly, inviting. They were telling her to follow.

She drifted into deep sleep.

A crash of thunder woke her.

She sat up—the house shook as the rumble of thunder continued, on and on. The sky was so dark, she figured it was still night. Then she noticed her alarm clock—the numbers flashed 6:58!

She jumped out of bed and had finished dressing when she remembered that today was Saturday. She let herself plop onto the bed.

An engine started up at the side of the house, and wheels backed over the gravel driveway. She leapt to the window. Who was driving the van at this time on Saturday morning, in the middle of a thunderstorm?

She met Ricky on the landing, still in his pajamas.

"Where're you going?" he asked.

She was fully dressed, she realized, as if she were about to go out.

"Nowhere. Who's in the van?"

"I dunno."

"But I heard it leave!"

"I don't know!"

"Quiet out there!" Jack yelled from his room. "I'm trying to sleep."

She went downstairs, Ricky close behind. All the hall lights were on. The door to Mom and Dad's room had been left open—she saw their unmade bed. In the kitchen, they found Ron eating a bowl of cereal.

"What's going on?" Lu said.

Ron put his spoon down.

"Dad drove Mom to the hospital."

"Is she okay?" she asked.

"Not sure," Ron said. "Dad said the baby was arriving too early and they wanted to stop it."

Lu sat on a chair. If Mom delivered the baby now, it'd be a preemie. Lu had heard about premature births—babies who were kept in intensive care, with tubes and monitors and specially heated cribs. What a way to start a life.

And some of them had all kinds of problems that didn't go away.

She wrapped her arms around herself.

And what about Mom?

"I want breakfast," Ricky said.

"Get it yourself," she snapped.

Ron looked up from his bowl.

"Toast or cereal?"

Ricky said "toast" in a quiet voice. Too late, Lu realized that he was scared, too. He walked over to the living room and turned on the TV, letting the frantic music of some cartoon fill the quiet. Ron popped two slices of bread into the toaster and eyed his sister.

"Want some, too?" he asked.

He was trying to smooth things over, in his own way.

"No thanks."

She had no appetite at all.

"What do we do?" she said.

"Wait," Ron said. "Dad said he'd call, and not to worry. They'll be fine."

Not worrying was much easier said than done.

The morning dragged. She went into Mom and Dad's room and made their bed. She saw the little cradle, still unassembled, leaning against one wall. What were Mom and Dad going to do if the baby was born and there was no cradle?

The phone rang around eleven—but it was just a kid in Jack's play. Jack didn't talk for more than five minutes, but what if he had been on too long? What if Dad was trying to call, at that very moment? What if Jack wasn't paying attention to the beep that said a call was waiting?

But Dad didn't phone until half past noon. Ron picked up. "Dad!" Ricky and Lu ran to the phone. Ron uh-huh-ed and nodded and hung up—he didn't give anyone else a chance.

"No fair!" Lu said. "I wanted to speak to him, too."

"You'll get to," Ron said. "He's coming home."

"What about Mom?" Jack asked.

"She's been admitted. They're giving her drugs to prevent contractions. They expect her to be there for a few days."

"When will Dad be home?" Ricky asked.

"In a couple of hours," Ron said, "to get stuff for Mom. Everything is okay."

Everything was not okay. Mom was in the hospital—at least for a few days, Dad had said. With a month and a half left before her due date, what if the drugs didn't work?

Lu's life seemed to be on hold. She had spent the morning waiting for Dad's call. She spent the afternoon waiting for his return home. Around three, the van pulled into the driveway. She ran to the door.

"How's Mom?" she asked.

"She feels fine," Dad said. "Mostly bored."

How come Mom was bored when everyone else was so scared?

"Can we see her?"

"Of course," Dad said.

Lu helped Dad gather things for Mom: a novel, a notepad, the newspaper, a few extra clothes, some toiletries, her hairbrush. Lu rushed—she wanted to be at the hospital.

"Slow down," Dad said. "Mom's not going anywhere."

They didn't leave the house until some time after four.

The hospital rules allowed only two visitors per patient, but they all snuck in anyway. The nurse assigned to Mom's room didn't seem to mind.

Mom was hooked up to tubes and plastic bags filled with clear liquid. She wore a hospital gown that didn't fit, and her hair looked a mess. But she lit up when she saw the family. Lu gave her a huge hug.

"I love you, too," Mom said.

While Mom and Dad talked about housekeeping and phone calls, Ricky pressed one button after another, making the head and then the foot of Mom's bed go up and down. Jack hummed a song from his play. Ron sat with Lu, next to Mom, watching Mom's animated face. The nurse poked her head in.

"Who pressed the call button?"

Mom and Dad turned to Ricky, who squirmed.

"I'm sorry," Mom said. "It won't happen again."

"No more buttons, young man," Dad said.

"Sorry," Ricky said.

He sounded it, too. Dad glanced at his watch.

"It's almost suppertime. How about I take you down to the cafeteria for some food?"

"Yeah!" Ricky said.

"Anyone else want to come?"

Jack and Ron stood. Lu didn't want to leave Mom's side.

"I'm not hungry," Lu said.

Mom looked from her to Dad.

"Take the boys. Lu can share some of mine."

Dad hesitated.

"I'll make sure she eats," Mom said.

After they left, Lu didn't know what to do. What do you tell someone who's laid up in the hospital? Mom picked up her brush.

"Can you brush my hair?"

Lu was grateful for the assignment. She climbed next

to Mom and began the slow process of untangling her thick hair.

"How's the house holding up?" Mom asked.

"Okay."

She didn't know what else to say. Mom shut her eyes as Lu pulled apart a set of snarls.

"Am I hurting you?"

"Nope," she said. "It feels good."

Once the knots came loose, brushing was easier. Lu braided her hair down her back. Mom lifted her hand to feel the braid and smiled. Lu's stomach tightened. The gesture was so familiar. It reminded her of when she was little and would watch Mom at the mirror, getting ready to go out. And here Mom was, stuck in such an awful place.

"Mom—"

She stopped. She stared at the brush.

"It's okay," Mom said. "You can ask."

"Are you really all right?"

Mom nodded.

"I think so. I was becoming dehydrated, and there's an imbalance in my blood. But . . ." She pointed to the bags and tubes. "They're taking care of that."

"What about the baby?"

Mom's smile grew.

"Hale and hearty. About five pounds already!"

Lu didn't know what that meant, but from Mom's expression, she knew this was good news.

"So you're coming home?"

"In a few days," Mom said. "They took pictures of the baby. Want to see?"

"Pictures?"

"Ultrasound." Of course. Lu knew about that. Sound waves were bounced off the baby, and a computer interpreted the image. "Take a look in my nightstand," Mom added.

Lu found several pieces of paper in the drawer showing the profile of a baby's head. The background was black, and only outlines in white were visible. She noticed something strange in the baby's mouth.

"What's that?" she asked.

"That's her thumb," Mom said.

The information didn't make any sense for a minute. The baby was sucking her thumb in the womb? *Her* thumb? The baby was a GIRL?!

"I'm going to have a sister!" Lu shrieked.

Mom laughed.

"Not for another month, I hope."

The car ride home was noisy but pleasant. Ricky talked nonstop about the EKG machine they had seen. The technician had explained to him how it worked.

"It makes the coolest graphs," Ricky was saying.

Lu smiled. Nothing was as cool as the pictures of her little sister.

# 25–Salman Page

### Bringing in the harvest

Saturday evening, Tina returned from the hospital exhausted. She had spent the day with Ozzy.

"He's mad as heck," she said. "Keeps saying someone tripped him. There's just no reasoning with him."

She was ready to return to him Sunday morning. A brisk breeze blew billowing clouds across the sun. Tina paused in the doorway.

"It'll frost tonight," she said. "Harvest what's left on the vines, Salman."

Tina's weather sense always amazed Salman. She hadn't checked the TV. They didn't have a newspaper. Yet she knew that it would frost. Salman no longer questioned the accuracy of her predictions.

After having spent Saturday cooped up because of the driving rain, Salman didn't mind this latest chore. His ankle had just about healed and he wanted to be outdoors. He began gathering the last of the tomatoes and peppers and squash. There were so many. He harvested for almost an hour when a call startled him.

"Salman!"

Lu waved to him from across the stream. Her cheeks glowed red. Salman's heart leapt. He walked down to her.

"Come on over," he said. "I'm alone."

Lu hesitated but then crossed the stream over the stones.

"I have news!" she said.

Salman had never seen her this out of breath. She must have run all the way.

"What's up?"

"Mom's having a girl! I'm going to have a sister."

Salman smiled. "For sure?"

"I saw the ultrasound," Lu said. "She's really cute."

"That's great!"

Lu's breathing slowed. She stared all around.

"This garden is huge," she said.

Salman nodded.

"I'm harvesting what's left, before tonight."

"By yourself?"

Salman nodded again.

"That's crazy," Lu said. "You can't do it all yourself."

Salman shrugged. What was there to say?

"Can I help you?" she asked.

"Sure!"

Salman found Lu a pair of gardening gloves that weren't too cruddy and showed her where they kept the bushel baskets.

"Just pick the nicest vegetables," he said. "We're not going to get everything."

They worked side by side. Not only did the picking go faster, but Salman filled the bushel baskets higher since he now had someone to help him carry the load. And Lu was there—solid, quiet company. He watched her saw off a large Hubbard squash from the vine, comfortable using the work knife he had lent her. She had strength and coordination.

"What are you going to do with all these veggies?" she asked.

She had perched the Hubbard on the top of the basket they were carrying together.

"Eat them," Salman said.

She laughed. He laughed, too, seeing the mounds accumulating in the trailer.

"Tina will can them first," Salman explained.

They emptied the basket and walked back to the garden.

"She's your foster mother?" Lu said.

"Yup."

"You get along with her?"

For a split second Salman wanted to change the subject. His instincts told him to keep quiet. But this was Lu. His d.b.

No, he corrected. His friend.

"She's okay," he said. "It's Ozzy I have trouble with."

"Ozzy?"

"Her husband." Salman paused. "My foster father."

The words tasted strange on his tongue.

And then, as they gathered rows of late beans, Salman told Lu about his first few weeks with the Royals, his night spent in the root cellar, how Ozzy watched everything Salman did, everything he took, made Salman feel like a thief.

Lu glanced at the trailer.

"I wouldn't want to meet him," she said.

"Don't worry. You won't."

He told her how Ozzy had been hospitalized.

"Wow," Lu said. "And my mom's in the hospital, too."

"Ozzy's in the veterans' hospital. He can't walk yet."

Lu avoided his gaze. She was embarrassed by her fear, Salman could tell.

"How is your mom, anyway?"

Relieved at the new subject, Lu told Salman everything that had happened in the last day.

"She says she'll be okay, but she didn't look right."

"No one looks right hooked up to tubes," Salman said.

"Yeah . . . But it's more than that. I'm not exactly sure. We see her again, later this afternoon."

Lu and Salman had harvested almost two-thirds of the garden when Salman's stomach began growling, hard.

"Want some lunch?" he asked.

"Sure."

Salman felt a little uncomfortable letting Lu into the trailer. She had been in it earlier, of course, to drop off the baskets, but now he was asking her to sit down.

"How about cooked tomatoes and rice?"

"Okay," Lu said.

He dug out the ingredients from the fridge and threw them into a pot. Within a few minutes they were bubbling.

"Smells good," she said.

Salman filled two bowls.

"Let's eat on the stoop."

Although the air was cool, the sun warmed him, and the steaming bowl heated his hands. There was just enough room on the step for the two of them to sit side by side. Salman felt Lu's warmth, too.

"It's a good thing you came," he said. "I'd never have finished this on my own."

"The work feels good," Lu said.

It did.

Salman washed the bowls, and they returned to harvesting. They were among the rows of summer squash when Lu paused and stared at the trailer. Salman reached down for a large zucchini.

"Have you *ever* had a real family?" she asked.

Salman froze momentarily before cutting the squash from the vine. Why was she asking him that?

She seemed to have asked herself the same question, because she shook her head and quickly began picking again.

"You don't need to answer. . . ."

"It's okay," Salman said.

Lu had told him about her mother and her sister-to-be and her brothers and her friends. She had shared herself, without his asking, giving of herself—time, advice, help—every time he saw her. And she had never asked for anything in return. Maybe he could trust her with Emolia Brown.

Salman placed another zucchini in the basket and straightened.

"There was a woman, once. My first foster home. I stayed there till I was almost six."

"She was family?"

Salman thought for a moment. He had called her Mama, and she had called him "my little boy."

"She's the one who chose my name."

"You mean Salman?"

He nodded.

"She said that there was this great Indian writer with that name."

Emolia had had to explain that she meant Indian from India. She had pulled out a map of the world to show him. That was the day he learned that perhaps his parents, too, had once come from there. And from then on, in the piles of books she borrowed from the library, she always had a few about South Asia.

"She said maybe I'd be a writer, too," Salman added.

He remembered sitting on her lap as she read him one book after another—books filled with colors and people and animals and even make-believe. "You'll write one of these books someday," she had said. And he believed her.

"Was she Indian, too?"

He shook his head.

"African American."

He couldn't recall her face anymore—but he never forgot her dark brown eyes and her large, warm arms, where he knew he was safe and loved.

He never had a South Asian foster parent. The state had placed him with white folks, brown ones, tan—from everywhere but India. He had wondered, growing up, how things would have been different if, just once, his foster parents had come from that part of the world.

"What happened to her?" Lu asked.

"She died," Salman said.

One day, after Emolia had dropped him off at kindergarten, a big truck hit the car she was driving. The semi's brakes had failed. The driver had tried to avoid her and couldn't. But Salman wasn't able to say those words. Not even to Lu. They still hurt.

"I'm sorry," Lu said.

"Not your fault." He went back to picking vegetables.

"Wasn't your fault, either."

Salman shrugged. But somewhere inside, he knew this was true. He looked at Lu. She was staring at him with a soft smile, as if to say, "You really are okay, you know." He averted his eyes but couldn't help smiling, too. Having Lu there, sharing part of him with her, felt good.

Soon after, Lu told Salman she had to leave.

"Meet you for lunch tomorrow," she said. "Okay?"

"Okay."

He was sorry to see her go. He felt lonely now, without her. Odd, since he hadn't felt lonely before she arrived.

He was lugging in the last basket when Tina pulled up in the pickup. She cut the engine but did not come out. Salman put the basket down and waited. A minute passed. She wasn't coming out. Salman reached down to lift the basket once again when he heard the click of the truck door opening. Tina seemed to drag herself out of the cab.

She had been crying. Her eyes were ringed in red, and she blew her nose before approaching him. She lowered her hulk onto the stoop, the same spot where Salman and Lu had shared lunch.

"Ozzy don't want you."

She said this with surprise. Salman's heart sank. Of course Ozzy didn't want him. Why didn't *she* know? Why did she have to go and tell him?

"It's been eating him up inside, he says. You underfoot." She shook her head. "I think it's just that he's so
low 'cause of his leg. When he can walk again, he'll come
'round."

Tina patted Salman on the cheek, to reassure him, he
assumed.

"You'll see. He'll come 'round."

Salman knew better.

# 26–Puck

### Calling a bluff

The queen wore the golden circlet on her perfect wrist. She rubbed its surface with a thumb, her only sign of distress.

"Tell me, Puck, has Oberon expressed any feelings for the boy?"

A strange question, I thought. And a dangerous one, I wagered.

"He dislikes him."

She raised an eyebrow.

"For the boy's sake or mine?"

I thought for a moment. Oberon had never said anything in particular about the boy, other than he disliked him because of the queen's attention.

"Yours, milady."

She nodded.

"Yet he has sent me an unusual message, Puck."

I waited. The queen would tell me in time. I didn't relish the knowledge.

"He has asked me to bring the boy to our world—to join our court."

"To destroy him?"

"No." She said this flatly, with certainty. "The message was clear. He swore no ill will. He wishes to provide the boy with the education of a prince—one the child deserves given my affections for him. The king would do him no harm, now or ever."

This was so absurd, I laughed.

"I do not see the humor, Puck."

"The boy is almost fifteen human years old. He is tall and hints at a beard. He has lost that innocent beauty of children which we so treasure. Even with the grace you have bestowed him, he would lay mockery to all we hold dear at court."

What possessed me? But it was all truth. Human babes and young children are fine companions. But almost-men? It would be an insult to Faery!

The queen seemed surprised but not angered.

"Does Oberon know this?" she asked.

"Yes. He has seen him."

She leaned back and pursed her lips.

"The king is calling my bluff."

It appeared so. I kept quiet, hoping I could be left out of it, for once.

That was not my luck.

"Perhaps it is time I settled this." She removed the circlet and handed it to me. I swallowed. I did not want the bracelet back.

"You shall deliver a message, Puck."

I would have swallowed again, but my mouth had run dry.

"Bring the circlet to the king. Tell him that he may bestow it on the boy when he delivers him to Faery."

She leaned back, and her smile was cold and cruel. "*If* he delivers him to Faery."

# 27 – Blos Pease

### Where is Salman?

Blos had always divided the kids at school between those he must avoid and those who avoided him. Until last year.

Last year, he had been assigned a d.b., the same d.b. as Lu Zimmer—Elaine Egger, one of the most popular girls in school.

Popular kids made Blos feel queasy. They never wanted to be near him. They made fun of him. Most avoided him.

But Elaine Egger decided to be a great d.b.—the best d.b. that ever was. That is what she told him. The first day of school she gave Blos and Lu a tour. She ate lunch with them the entire first week. She met with Blos once a month, for the entire school year, to see how he was doing, she said. She gave him a Halloween card, a Christmas card, and a Valentine's Day card. And best of all, she kept all the eighth-grade popular kids from bothering him.

Seventh grade had been the best.

And Lu had become his friend. Or, at least, she did not avoid him. Especially after Frances Drummond left.

This year, Salman Page had entered his life. Salman smiled when he saw Blos. Salman asked him to stay. He had laughed at Blos's joke! Not only did Salman not avoid Blos, Salman welcomed him.

So when Salman did not show up on Monday, Blos noticed.

"Where is Salman?" he asked.

Lu, who had taken out a sandwich from her lunch bag, glanced at the lunch line.

"I think his class let out late."

"No," Blos said. "I saw other kids in line."

Lu's eyes darted around the cafeteria as she bit into her sandwich. Her eyebrows furrowed. She put her sandwich down and swallowed.

"After lunch we'll look for him, okay?" she said.

Blos nodded. Lunch. He concentrated on that. His mom had told him once that certain foods came in a certain order. Like a pyramid. The base had grains. Then fruits, vegetables, protein, and then dessert. Dessert was always last. Blos lined it up: a roll with peanut butter, apple slices, cut carrots, hard-boiled egg whites, and a cookie. Peanut butter was a legume, but Mom had told him it was almost like a grain. They could be eaten together.

What he really wanted was the cookie. But that came last. He had better eat fast.

Lu was still chewing her sandwich when Blos finished.

"I will go check the classrooms," Blos said.

"You can't check all the classrooms," Lu said.

Blos paused and glanced at his watch. He had fifteen minutes. Lu was right. He could not check all the classrooms and make it to World History on time.

"Either he's called in sick," Lu continued, "he's in detention, or he's in the nurse's office."

Why had he not thought of that? Lu crammed the rest of her food into her bag.

"I'll check with the nurse and at detention. Why don't you go to the office and ask if he's been called in absent?"

Blos nodded. He watched Lu pitch her bag right into the center of the nearest garbage can. He got up slowly. He really, truly did not want to speak with Ms. Esterschultz, the school secretary. If anyone made him queasy, she did.

Lu was already out the door, and Blos plodded in her wake.

The office was just around the corner from the

cafeteria. A big glass window surrounded it. Behind Ms. Esterschultz's desk was the principal's office. Blos gulped.

Lu had asked him, though. And he had nodded. Nodding was the same as saying "yes." And Salman was not in school—at least, not at lunch. Blos pushed the door open with sweaty palms.

Ms. Esterschultz was not at her desk. Blos breathed a sigh of relief.

He spun around, ready to run, and crashed into Ms. Esterschultz as she entered from a side door that led to the teachers' lounge.

"Mr. Pease," she said, "please be careful!"

"Sorry," Blos mumbled.

"What are you doing here?"

Blos looked at his shoes.

"Well?"

"Um . . ." Blos cleared his throat. He kept his eyes on his sneakers. "Is Salman Page absent?"

Ms. Esterschultz huffed.

"No one called to say he'd be. But you can check with his homeroom teacher."

Blos's mind went blank. Who was Salman's homeroom teacher? He concentrated on his shoelaces. Had Salman ever told him?

Ms. Esterschultz sighed.

"Ms. Rabinowitz," she said.

"Thank you," Blos mumbled.

He ran. He ran all the way to Mr. Loengredl's classroom. Blos positioned himself in the front of the room. He turned his notebook to today's page. He placed his history book to the left, his four-color pen, his pencil, his eraser, and his ruler in a line above. He glanced at his watch. Six minutes.

Ms. R's class was two flights down. He could not make it there and back. But he had her after Mr. Loengredl. He would ask her then.

An out-of-breath Lu popped her head in the door, holding her side.

"I thought you might be here," she said.

Where else would he be? Blos wondered. Lu exhaled and shook her head.

"Salman's not in detention, or at the nurse's office. What'd Ms. Esterschultz say?"

"She did not know," Blos said. "She said Ms. R should."

"I have her now," Lu said. "I'll ask her."

Blos nodded.

"Next time," Lu continued, "come tell me, okay?"

"Okay."

She ran off. Blos was puzzled. Next time? He clicked his pen to green. The bell rang. He spent the rest of the afternoon taking down what his teachers said, word for word.

At the end of the day, Lu was waiting at the bus line. She did not take the bus. Why was she in line?

"Blos," Lu said, "he wasn't in. He never showed."

Blos stared at Lu. What was she talking about?

"How about we go see how he's doing?" she continued.

"See how who is doing?"

"Salman," Lu said. "Maybe he can use some cheering up."

Blos did not know how to cheer people up. He had never been asked to.

"Well . . ."

"We can meet at the stream by the garden. Okay?"

Blos felt more and more bewildered.

"When?" he asked.

"As soon as you make it home."

Blos stared at her. Other kids were staring, too. Lu had asked him to meet her. He could not recall anyone ever asking him to meet outside of school.

"Okay," he said.

Blos felt queasy the entire ride home. But there was an excitement there, too. And this kind of excitement did not feel bad—just new.

# 28 – Lu-Ellen Zimmer

### Canning

Lu reached the foot of the Royals' garden, arguing with herself. So Salman had been home sick. Kids missed school all the time. Yet she wanted to see him. Why, then, had she asked Blos to be there, too? Maybe because she wanted to see Salman too much and she needed Blos as an excuse? Lame, Lu told herself, she was being lame.

She shook away that uncomfortable thought and watched the Royals' trailer from across the stream. A parked pickup truck stuck out behind the trailer. Salman's foster parents must be home. Somehow, she hadn't thought of that. She didn't want to meet them.

Blos ran up, his hair wilder than ever.

"I came right over," he said. "I did not eat a snack."

A screen door slammed.

"Shhh," Lu said.

Blos jerked his head toward the trailer. The truck shifted, as if something had been dropped into it, then started up with a cough. It rolled away.

"Do you think Salman has left?" Blos asked.

Smoke billowed out of a small chimney.

"I don't know," Lu said.

The screen door slammed again. A few seconds later, Salman appeared carrying a heaping bucket, which he dumped at the side of the garden.

"Salman!" Blos yelled.

Salman looked up. Lu stood next to Blos, making herself visible.

"Blos! Lu! Come on over."

They crossed the stream and met Salman at the top of the garden.

"You were not at school," Blos said.

"Is that why you're here?" Salman asked.

Blos nodded. Lu reddened.

"We were wondering if you were sick or something," she said.

"Tina needed help with canning," Salman said. "There was too much for one person."

He headed back to the trailer.

"Come in. Tina's gone to see Ozzy. She won't be back for a few hours."

Lu almost keeled over when she walked in, with all that heat and steam and the overwhelming smell of cooked vegetables. Her glasses fogged up. After she wiped them on her shirt, she noticed the jars.

They filled the trailer. Crowded every flat surface.

"You can roast in this roost," Blos said.

Salman grinned. Blos did, too, proud.

"It does get hot in here," Salman said. "I still have a batch of tomatoes to can."

Lu had trouble hearing Salman over the noise. The stove fan whirred full blast, sucking up steam that was percolating from pots at every burner.

"Can I watch?" Blos asked.

Salman washed and quartered tomatoes while answering Blos's questions about the workings of the pressure cookers. Lu stared at the jars—dozens of oversized jewels in oranges and reds and greens. She stepped closer to the yellow ones on the table, admiring the shiny, translucent seeds, when Salman startled her.

"Blos is watching the pressure gauges," he said.

She hadn't heard him approach. She caught her breath.

"The jars," she said, "they're . . ."

She stopped.

"Beautiful," Salman said, completing her thought. "I think so, too."

"They have all reached ten pounds!" Blos cried.

"Turn down the heat," Salman said. "Be right there."

Salman glanced at her before he checked the flame under each pot—gave her a little happy shiver.

"Good job," he told Blos. "Now we leave them cooking for forty-five minutes."

"Oh."

Blos deflated like a balloon.

"You can help me tighten yesterday's jars," Salman said.

That perked Blos back up. Salman returned to the table with a sheet of white stickers. Someone had printed *Yellow Squash* and the date on them. When they finished tightening and labeling, Salman checked the pressure cookers again.

"Can you help me carry these to the root cellar?" Salman said. "It'll be quicker."

Lu's heart raced. The root cellar. She had visions of chains and evil hooded dungeon masters. Salman must have read her thoughts.

"It's okay in the daylight," he said.

Lu wondered whether he saw her embarrassment as well. She hurriedly picked up two jars. Salman took three, then led them 'round the chicken coop to where the land dropped. A door had been built in the hollow, under the small hill. He unlatched it and they entered a dark, cool cave filled with shelves.

"We put them here," Salman said.

He placed the jars on one of the few empty shelves

near the bottom. Lu marveled at the row upon row of preserves, all the shades of a rainbow.

"How do you keep track of what's in here?"

"I don't," Salman said. "But Tina can tell you what these shelves hold, down to the date each jar was sealed."

Lu whistled.

After returning from their third trip to the root cellar, Blos pointed to the remaining jars on the table.

"We move these, too?"

"Nope," Salman said. "Not till tomorrow. They have to cool and settle first."

Although they had emptied half of the table, the trailer still seemed to be filled with jars. How did Salman plan to fit them all into the cellar?

Blos checked his watch.

"Forty-five minutes are up."

"Great," Salman said.

He turned off the burners and showed Blos how to remove the gauges.

"We let the steam escape," he said, "and wait awhile."

"Why don't you take the jars out?" Lu asked.

"The glass might crack," Blos said.

How did Blos know that?

Out the window, the afternoon light was beginning to fade. Lu realized, with some disappointment, that she needed to go.

"I have to head home soon," she said.

Blos glanced at his watch. "Me too."

"Thanks for coming," Salman said.

He held the door open and Blos stepped out. As Lu exited, she looked up at Salman. He was smiling down at her. She hesitated, ready to take a step closer, close enough to touch, but at that moment, the pickup that had left earlier pulled into the dirt driveway. Lu hurried down the steps. The screen door banged behind her.

A large woman slid out of the truck and scowled at them.

"Who's you got here?" she demanded.

"Some friends," Salman said.

"We just came to help," Lu said. Her heart was pounding hard in her chest. She saw Blos's eyes dart from side to side.

The woman's eyes narrowed. "I see."

"They were leaving," Salman said.

"Well then, go," the woman said.

Blos bolted. Lu followed more slowly, taking a second to wave. The woman didn't move.

When Lu reached the woods on the other side of the stream, Blos wasn't there. He must have run home. She sniffed. All that steam had made her nose runny.

She trudged back the way she had come. Why had Tina been so mean? she wondered. They hadn't done anything wrong. Lu shivered. How did Salman manage, living with such a woman?

She sniffed again.

# 29—Salman Page

## Rejects

Tina didn't move from her spot until Lu was completely out of sight.

"Who said you could have visitors?" she said.

"They're friends," Salman said.

"I saw you looking at that girl. It's more than friendship you want."

What business was it of Tina's? Salman thought. What business? He tightened his lips, afraid of what he might say.

"I don't want no rejects poking around," she continued.

"They're not rejects!"

She gave a hollow laugh.

"Says a body who's one himself."

Salman flinched but he didn't back down.

"You can't tell me who my friends are."

Tina straightened. Her eyes narrowed. Salman had never spoken to her like that before. But then, Tina had never treated him this way before, either.

"I can tell you who is and isn't allowed on my property," she said. "They isn't."

She lumbered into the house, pushing Salman aside.

Something was eating at her, and it was more than a couple of kids visiting the trailer, Salman knew. But he was too angry to care.

He stomped away.

He went down the hollow, past the chicken coop, to his maple tree. He climbed up and sat rigid against the trunk. His mind raced. She was the reject, not him. She and Ozzy. They had set themselves up in a part of town cut off from the rest, where no one went, as if they were afraid that someone might see what they were up to. Harvesting vegetables and raising chickens—in the most unbelievable jungle of a garden—but who cared?

Just 'cause they didn't want to be seen in public didn't mean Salman didn't have the right to have friends.

A cool breeze blew around him. He slipped his hands into his pants pockets to warm them and pulled out a piece of paper. He unfolded the photo of himself, Lu, and Bird that Blos had given him. Where was Bird? he wondered.

As if attuned to Salman's thoughts, the crow flew past and landed on top of the chicken coop, where he began to preen himself. A few chickens, unhappy with his presence, started making a fuss. Bird flew up next to Salman onto the branch. Salman patted his shirt pocket.

"'Fraid I don't have anything for you today," he said.

Bird stretched his neck as if to check the photo.

"Want to see it? It's pretty good."

Bird hopped closer, tilting his head from side to side.

"Blos wants to print it in the paper," Salman said. "What do you think?"

The crow tilted his head one more time, then hopped back. To Salman it looked exactly like a shrug. He laughed.

"Doesn't matter, huh?"

Bird cawed and flew down to peck at some chicken feed that had rolled to the foot of the tree.

Salman stared at the photo. The creases where he had folded it just missed Bird in the middle and the tops of Lu's and Salman's heads. He refolded it carefully, pain creeping in where he had vowed it never would.

He returned to the trailer after nightfall. Tina stood at the sink, washing the pots that had been used to cook vegetables and steam the filled mason jars. She spoke without turning.

"Ozzy'll be released on Friday."

Something cold ran down Salman's spine. Tina kept scrubbing the pots, well beyond the need. She rinsed and scrubbed some more.

"He still wants you out."

"I want to stay," Salman said.

He meant it.

Sitting in that tree, he had realized that he didn't want to go somewhere else. He didn't mind Tina, not too much, even if she had been mean. And though he hated Ozzy, he had no idea what was waiting for him at his next placement. But more important, despite everything, he had found friends. Real friends. People who cared about him and whom he cared about. He wasn't going to leave that. Never.

Tina turned toward him. She had been crying again. She didn't want him to go, either. Maybe there was hope.

"I'll talk to him," she said.

Salman picked up a dish towel and began drying the pots in the drain.

"Tomorrow," she said, "we work on Ozzy's fence."

Salman shivered.

# 30—Salman Page

### Absence note

Salman sat in the back row, copying Ms. R's newest essay assignment, which was as bizarre as her previous ones. "How do two people link up together to become friends? Provide a thesis, clear examples, and a strong argument."

Ms. R began explaining.

"You may use examples from books, your personal lives . . ."

The PA system crackled on.

"Mr. Salman Page, please come to the office."

Ms. R glanced at Salman. With barely a rustle, he stood, walked to the front, and took the hall pass from her. Out the door in fifteen seconds.

What did the office want?

Ms. Esterschultz was waiting for him, his school file on her desk.

"Mr. Page," she said, "you were absent Monday."

That was two days ago. He nodded.

"We don't have a note, Mr. Page. We need a reason for your absence."

Without thinking, Salman said, "I was canning."

"Canning?"

He could tell from her arched eyebrows that she didn't understand what he meant.

"Vegetables, ma'am. We brought in the harvest on Sunday."

"And you were required to can them?"

"Yes, ma'am."

"Instead of going to school?"

It dawned on him that this probably wasn't going to be an excuse she had heard before. One she might not approve of. Not that he cared whether she approved of the Royals, but this was going to attract attention.

"Yes, ma'am."

She puckered her lips into a frown. No. No question. She didn't approve.

"Mr. Page, did you volunteer for this?"

He shifted. There was no right answer to this question. Either he did and was truant, or he didn't and the Royals were unreasonable—at least from Ms. Esterschultz's point of view.

He concentrated on the lower half of her desk.

"I see," she said.

She drummed her fingers on his file.

"Next time, be sure your foster parents write you an absence note."

"Yes, ma'am."

He escaped as fast as he could. On his way to Ms. R's classroom he worried, though. What if Ms. Esterschultz contacted his social worker? Would she approve?

# 31 – Lu-Ellen Zimmer

### Big red letters

Stupid cold! Lu blew her nose for the twentieth time that morning. She'd caught a cold Monday evening and it didn't seem to be getting any better. Because of it, Dad didn't let her visit Mom.

"When you're healthier," he said. "We don't want Mom to catch anything."

He had said that Tuesday—three days ago. And Mom was still in the hospital. She was only supposed to be there for a few days, but almost a week had gone by, and they still hadn't discharged her.

Yesterday, Salman had tried to be reassuring.

"Everyone says she's improving, right?"

"Yeah."

"And they've told you your sister is just fine."

"True."

"Why would they lie to you?"

"They wouldn't," Lu admitted. "But Mom hasn't been discharged."

"She will."

Salman smiled when he said that. His smiles made Lu feel warm. She looked forward to them—to Salman.

Except they had fought after that. Salman told her that Ozzy was coming back.

"He treats you rotten," she said. "Can't you ask to go someplace else?"

"There's nowhere else to go," he said.

"There must be somewhere that isn't as awful."

Salman spoke to her as if she were pathetic.

"I'm almost fifteen. No one asks for grown boys."

I'd ask for you, she thought.

"We have a guest room. . . ."

"Your parents aren't going to want a foster kid. Especially not with a baby coming."

"My parents love kids."

"Well, good for you," Salman said.

He left the cafeteria with a scowl. Lu immediately regretted what she had said. She hadn't meant to hurt him. She hadn't thought how her words might sound to him.

She'd apologize today, she vowed. And this afternoon, she'd make Dad take her to the hospital to see Mom, cold or no cold.

She sat in Ms. R's classroom waiting for the school paper meeting to start. Kids were still wandering in. Blos sat up front, as usual. Salman wasn't here yet. Lu had a one-page piece ready, just as Ms. R had requested. It provided a glowing report of the designated buddy program. She had even interviewed Vice Principal Phillip: "The d.b. program is what distinguishes Springfalls from the other junior high schools in the area."

"Good morning," Ms. R said. "Our goal is to publish our first edition by the end of the month."

She asked students to tell her what they had written. Ruthie raised her hand.

"I wrote a piece about the band."

"Excellent. Why don't you read it to the group."

Ruthie turned bright red.

"Couldn't I just hand it in?"

Ms. R smiled.

"Your article will be read by the entire school. By reading it to us first, we'll get a chance to help you make it the best it can be."

"Okay," Ruthie said. But she didn't seem all that okay about it.

The piece only took a minute or two to read. It described what instruments were in the band, the practice schedule, the planned performance dates.

"That's very nice, Ruthie," Ms. R said. "Does anyone have any comments?"

Silence. Kids stared at each other. Then a boy Lu didn't know raised his hand.

"Yes, Richard," Ms. R said.

"I think I might want to know what it's like to play in the band."

"What do you mean?"

"I guess it might be nice if a band member was interviewed, or the band leader, and we got an idea of what a member has to do."

Ms. R nodded. "What do you think, Ruthie?"

Ruthie crinkled her chin.

"I didn't think of that." She paused briefly. "Can I interview myself? I'm a band member."

"What do others think?" Ms. R said.

"Reporters are supposed to be objective," Richard said. "Ruthie can't be objective about herself."

Lu wondered about that. After all, her piece was for a photo of her and Salman. Another girl—Lu thought her name was Susan—jumped in.

"Reporters are never *really* objective, no matter what they say. Why can't Ruthie talk about her own experiences, if she's up-front about what she's doing?"

Ms. R nodded to each student in turn. Lu listened to the discussion intently but didn't join in. The half hour was almost up, and Salman hadn't showed.

The first bell rang.

"Excellent discussion," Ms. R said. "Please hand in

your columns before you leave, and I'll get back to you with comments before next Friday."

Blos approached Ms. R as everyone was leaving.

"I only have pictures."

"That's plenty," Ms. R said.

She went through the prints Blos handed her.

"You have a good eye," she said.

He tapped his right cheek.

"My right one," he said, and fled.

Lu smiled at his literalness. She handed in her piece and wondered where Salman was. He was late. Maybe Tina had made him do some more canning. Lu'd see him at lunch.

But Salman wasn't at lunch, either. Blos looked as puzzled as Lu felt.

"Should we meet at his place?" he asked.

Out the window, the gray skies of this morning had opened into rain. Wind sent leaves swirling almost horizontal.

"It's kind of nasty to be out," she said.

Blos nodded.

"Tomorrow," she said.

"Okay."

Besides, she thought, she had to see Mom.

As she gathered her pack after lunch, Rob and Sean walked by. Sean elbowed Rob in the arm. Rob grinned and stopped.

"Well, if it isn't the Bird Tamer," Rob said.

Lu ignored them. She shouldered her pack and began walking toward Ms. R's class. Rob and Sean followed.

"The loon's still hooked pretty tight," Sean said.

"Lost the chicken, though," Rob said.

"He flew the coop."

"She must have given him the wrong scratch."

Both laughed. Lu walked faster.

"You'll have to find another chicken," Rob said. "Yours has been roasted for good."

Lu whirled.

"What does that mean?"

Surprised by her fury, Rob raised his hands, as if to ward her off.

"He's been transferred out," he said. "Didn't you know?"

"No. When?"

"Don't know. I saw his file this morning when I got a pass from the office."

"So? Files are out for all kinds of reasons."

"Not with a note that says RETURN TO STATE in big red letters on 'em."

Was he telling the truth? She stared at Rob just long enough for him to avert his eyes. Then she pushed between the boys and headed back to the office.

The school secretary was on the phone when Lu walked in. Lu eyed the piles on her desk. In a bin marked "FOR PICK-UP" she saw three large manila envelopes and a smaller white one. Did one of those envelopes contain Salman's file?

Ms. Esterschultz hung up.

"Yes, Ms. Zimmer?"

"I've been told that Salman Page has been transferred. Is that true?"

Ms. Esterschultz smiled one of her aren't-you-a-nice-girl-to-be-concerned-about-something-like-that smiles. Lu hated adults who did that.

"Why do you want to know?"

"I'm his d.b.," Lu said.

Ms. Esterschultz nodded.

"Of course. Yes, the state called this morning and informed me that he's leaving the school district."

"Do you know where he's going?"

"No. But even if I did, I couldn't tell you. I'm not permitted to disclose other students' records to you."

Lu could tell she was trying to be kind, even if she was no help at all.

"Thank you, Ms. Esterschultz."

Lu left the office and crumpled onto the bench by the office door.

Salman was gone. Ms. Esterschultz wasn't able to tell her where.

This couldn't be happening.

She had lost Frances—and a friendship she had taken for granted since kindergarten. But then she had connected with Salman. And somehow, he had helped her connect with Blos. She got abuse for that. From every-one, it seemed. But even so, Salman was her friend. A real friend. Someone she liked who liked her in return. Just thinking about him, right then, made her happy. She wasn't going to lose him, too. She wouldn't let that happen.

The more she thought about Salman, the more she realized that he was going to lose her, too. He'd spent his life moving from place to place. He had no family. His best placement had been with a woman who died when he was five years old. He needed a friend. Someone who wouldn't give up on him just 'cause he had to move again. Someone like her.

But how was she going to find him? Not by sitting in this hallway, that was for sure.

She went to her locker and put on her jacket and cap. Someone had to know where Salman was. He was a boy, not some trash you threw away. She was going to figure this out.

The bell rang, and kids started rushing to classes. She crossed Rob as she headed out the door.

"Where're you going, Bird Tamer?" he asked.

She glared at him, and he wilted, if only for a second. Then she left. She had more important things to do.

# 32 – Lu-Ellen Zimmer

### Beaten down and withered

The rain blew into Lu's face as she walked home. She'd go to the Royals' trailer. Maybe Salman was still there. She dropped her pack by the back door and headed for the woods, which appeared forbidding in the storm. But she knew that once she reached the trees, the rain wouldn't come down as hard.

She picked her way through fallen branches, brushed past dripping bushes, and finally made it to the creek. She followed its swollen course, taking note of the rough whitecaps as it flowed next to her. At the foot of Salman's garden, she tried to cross where the stones jutted out, but she slipped and landed on her knees in cold water. Water rushed around her, threatening to pull her down, but she pushed herself up quickly and splashed across to the other side. Her boots were waterlogged. Her pants, soaked. Her jacket, wet almost to the chest. And instead of an easy path through the garden, she ran into a six-foot-high chicken-wire fence strung between stakes.

No fence was going to stop her!

She decided to circle the property: she'd follow the bushes along the edge of the garden and, at the first gap, she'd cross through.

She trudged along, her feet and legs chilled. The rain was letting up a bit, but the wind gusted relentlessly. She ran into a thicket of mountain laurel and thought she was lost, when she saw a large maple tree and, above it, the back of the chicken coop.

She climbed the small hill to the front of the trailer. A light shone inside and a TV flickered.

She did not want to speak with Tina but she had no choice. She knocked.

Seconds dragged. She was about to knock again when she heard someone unfasten the dead bolt. The door cracked open, the chain still on. Tina squinted out at her.

"What are you doing here?"

Lu shivered on the stoop. Tina looked at her for a second longer, shut the door to unhook the chain, and reopened it, wide.

"Come in," she said. "You're near frozen."

"Thanks," Lu said.

The trailer was warm. Lu's glasses, streaked with rain, fogged up. She tried to wipe them with her sleeve. A man sat on the sofa in front of the TV, one of his legs encased in a cast propped up on the coffee table. He looked like a beached sea lion—if beached sea lions ·wore clothes, drank beer, and smoked cigarettes.

"Who's this?" he demanded.

"A friend of Salman's," Tina said.

"Well, he's gone."

That must be Ozzy. Lu didn't want any trouble.

"Sorry to bother you . . . ," she said. She placed her hand on the doorknob.

"It's okay, hon," Tina said. "You're looking for him, right?"

Lu nodded. She noticed Tina's puffy eyes and red nose.

"Tell the critter to get out," Ozzy growled.

"She ain't no critter," Tina snapped.

Lu opened the door a crack. Tina put a hand on her arm.

"I'm sorry, hon. DCF picked him up this morning."

"I told 'em to," Ozzy said.

Tina winced. Lu hadn't expected to feel sorry for her, but she realized that she did. Anyone could see that this woman hadn't wanted Salman to leave. Maybe she had liked Salman, in her own way. Maybe she wasn't all bad. And she was stuck with someone like Ozzy.

"Do you know where Salman's gone?" Lu asked.

"Nope. DCF won't tell me."

Tina sniffed.

"Is there someone I can speak to at . . ."

Lu couldn't remember the initials.

"DCF," Tina said. "I have his social worker's number. You can have it."

"Please," Lu said.

Tina went to the kitchen counter and pulled open a drawer. She rummaged around.

"Why ain't she gone yet?" Ozzy demanded.

"She's going, she's going," Tina said.

She returned to Lu, a business card in her hand.

"Here. I don't need it anymore."

Lu took the card. On it was printed "Paula Lloyd, MSW, Department of Children and Families." An address and phone number were printed at the bottom.

"Thanks," she said.

"Don't thank us, just get out!" Ozzy said.

Lu skittered out the door. When she reached the bottom step, Tina exited, too.

"Wait."

Lu stopped. Tina stepped down, hugging herself in the rain.

"If you speak to him, can you tell him I'm sorry? I'm not the best foster mother, but I really tried."

Lu nodded. She attempted to swallow the lump in her throat.

"I'll tell him."

She watched Tina climb back up the stairs. She turned once in the doorway and waved. Lu wasn't sure whether rain was rolling down Tina's cheeks or tears. Lu waved back. As she left, the dead bolt clicked.

In the few minutes Lu had spent in the trailer, the rain had picked up and the wind had only become stronger. The garden looked beaten down and withered, as if whatever had made it blossom and grow had vanished. She rounded the chicken coop, heading down the hollow, when a gust pummeled her. She bent forward, clutching her hat, and heard a loud *crack* from the maple across from the coop. A large limb came crashing down. She jumped back, her heart racing.

The trees all around were whipping in the wind. A smaller branch dangled off another maple farther down. She took a deep breath and stepped forward. Then a bird—was it a crow?—flew across her path, frightening her even more, making her jolt back again.

She wasn't safe in the forest.

She scrambled around to the front of the trailer. She'd have to use the roads. She pulled her jacket tighter, pushed her hat further down over her ears.

She walked, head down, out the dirt and gravel driveway, now a river of mud, onto the small road. It, too, was lined with trees. She kept to the center, praying no car was going to knock her over. The first intersection was Route 51. If she followed it toward town, she'd hit Main

Street. Down Main Street about five blocks, and she'd reach the school, and then a few more blocks till home.

She turned toward town. Pretty soon, she began passing businesses. Because there were no sidewalks, she kept to the far side of the breakdown lane by the curb, crossing into parking lots when they edged up. She shivered. Her hat was soaked. Rain had begun seeping into the shoulders of her jacket. She couldn't feel her toes. But she kept walking.

She passed the Quick Stop and the PharmAid drugstore that Dad sometimes drove to. She placed one foot in front of the other, clutching her arms for warmth.

The water on her glasses blurred her vision, so she peered over them.

She reached the FillStar gas station, and her teeth were chattering so hard she couldn't keep her head still. She needed a place to stop. A place to sit. A place that was dry.

She lurched over to the building. It didn't have an entrance, only a booth where motorists paid through a thick window. She saw the attendant sitting in the light, reading something, bored. She knocked on his window. He looked up.

"Let . . . me . . . in . . . please."

The attendant shook his head and pointed to a sign. NO ADMITTANCE. EMPLOYEES ONLY. He looked back down at his paper.

No admittance. She wasn't an employee. She walked farther.

She passed a stand of trees. Everything was so gray, as if she were walking through unending twilight. Traffic whizzed by.

She passed a car dealership. Passed a small shopping mall. She'd have to turn into it to find a building—the parking lot was so wide. She needed to get to town. She continued, straight ahead. A light. An office building. A grocery store recessed behind another huge parking lot. One foot. Then another.

Then, almost as if it were a miracle, she saw a bus shelter: a bench surrounded on three sides by Plexiglas. It was empty. She stumbled in, huddled in the farthest corner, where the glass curved forward, giving extra shelter. The bench was dry. She lifted her legs, bent her knees, and hugged them to her chest. The walls blocked the wind.

Just a minute, she thought. She'd stay here just a minute. Just long enough for the shivering to stop.

She shut her eyes.

Just a minute.

## 33 – Blos Pease

**Something had happened to Lu**

Blos felt queasy all afternoon.

Salman was gone. And he had seen Lu leave, too. Right after lunch. He was alone, in a building full of kids who avoided him or whom he needed to avoid.

Blos missed an entire minute of Mr. Loengredl's lecture because of his worry. An entire minute! He left a blank line. But taking notes did not stop the gnawing in his belly.

As soon as the bus dropped him off at the end of the day, he ran to find the phone book.

Zimmer. Only one listed in Springfalls. Must be Lu's number. He called.

"Hello?" a boy answered.

"Can I please speak to Lu?"

"She's not in."

She had gone to find Salman. Blos knew.

"She is not back?" he said.

"Uh . . . no. Who is this?"

She was not in. It had been hours since lunch.

"Are you sure she is not back?" Blos said.

"Yes. Who *is* this?"

His queasiness grew. Something had happened to Lu.

"Hello? Are you still there?" The voice on the other end sounded different. Was it worried? Blos was.

"Yes," Blos said.

"Who are you?"

"Blos Pease."

"Lu hasn't called. Do you know where she is?"

"Yes."

Pause. Silence. He knew. He knew.

"Well, aren't you going to tell me?"

"She is at Salman's."

"The kid who she's d.b.-ing?"

"Yes."

"Well, that's okay."

No, it was not. Blos knew that, too.

"She needs help," Blos said.

He had to get her help. Lu needed Blos's help.

"Help for what?"

The new tone had become stronger.

"I do not know," Blos said.

A pause.

"Listen, I'm going to call my father. How can we reach you?"

"You can phone me."

"Where?"

Blos's queasiness had begun to take over. He croaked his phone number and hung up. How was he going to help Lu?

His mother was at work—she would be home in another hour. He was not supposed to call her unless he had an emergency. Was this an emergency?

He did not know what to do. The street was deep gray. The wind was blowing branches. The rain fell almost sideways. Then the phone rang.

Blos jumped. He listened to the phone ring a second time.

Pick it up, he told himself.

A third ring.

"Hello?" he said.

"Hi. Is this Blos Pease?"

A man's voice. On the other end of the line. A man Blos did not know.

"Yes."

"This is Tony Zimmer, Lu's father. My son Jack just called. He said you thought Lu needed help."

"Yes," Blos said.

"Do you know where she is?"

"Yes."

"Can you tell me?"

"Salman's house."

"Where is it?"

"I can show you."

"Where are you?"

"Five-zero-three Penny Lane."

"I'll be right over."

Blos sat in the living room, staring out the front window. Minutes crept by. A red van with its lights on slowly inched down the road. Lu's family's car! He had seen it before. Blos grabbed his coat to run outside.

He stopped at the threshold. He had forgotten to leave a note for Mom. She had told him that he should leave her a note if he went somewhere different than he usually did. But he had been to Salman's before. And the van was approaching. It might miss him if he did not wave. He needed it to find Lu.

Blos ran to the curb. The van pulled up. A window rolled down. A man, tall in his seat, with dark hair and wire glasses, leaned over.

"Are you Blos?"

Blos nodded.

"I'm Tony Zimmer. Hop in."

Blos opened the door. A strange car. His queasiness was powerful. He had trouble climbing in.

"Okay, Blos. Where are we going?"

Blos could not speak. His throat was all tied up. His hands shook.

"It's okay," Mr. Zimmer said. "Just point which way."

Blos pointed to the end of his street. Mr. Zimmer furrowed his brow.

"That's a dead end. Is she at the end of your street?"

Blos shook his head. He had to explain. Lu needed him to explain.

"In the woods," Blos said. "At the edge of the stream."

"She's in the woods?" Mr. Zimmer said.

Blos had to be clearer. He gripped the side handle on the door, steadying himself.

"No. The trailer is at the edge of the stream. The trucking property stream. On the town line."

"She's at a place on the edge of the trucking terminal property, you're saying, on the town line?"

Blos nodded. Mr. Zimmer pulled out a map and turned on the dome light.

"The trucking property covers hundreds of acres, Blos. Can you be a little more specific?"

"I can walk there in fifteen minutes," Blos said, opening the door.

Mr. Zimmer put a hand on Blos's other arm. Blos froze.

"Hold on, Blos. I think this map will help us."

Blos hesitated, then shut the door. Mr. Zimmer pointed to a large, irregular shape on the map.

"The property is here. Your street is here. And the town line is here."

Mr. Zimmer looked up and smiled.

"There's only one road that will fit the bill."

Mr. Zimmer drove down side streets. They turned onto Route 51 and took another right onto another street lined with trees—forests, it seemed to Blos.

"What does the house look like?" Mr. Zimmer said.

"It is a trailer."

Mr. Zimmer drove slowly. They passed a mud driveway. That was it!

"There!" Blos said.

Mr. Zimmer backed up and pulled into the driveway. Blos's queasiness was so strong, it took all of his concentration to breathe.

"Come on, Blos," Mr. Zimmer said. "Let's see if Lu's here."

They walked up to the front door, Mr. Zimmer leading. He knocked. A few seconds later, the door opened with the chain still on.

"Who is it?" a woman asked.

"I'm Tony Zimmer. I'm looking for my daughter, Lu. This young man thinks Lu might be here."

"She a skinny thing with glasses?" the woman said.

"That's one way to describe her," Mr. Zimmer said.

"Hold on." The woman shut the door, then immediately reopened it without the chain. "Come in," she said.

The place felt steamy. It smelled of cigarettes and alcohol. A man in front of the TV with his leg in a cast frowned at them.

"I'm sorry to bother you," Mr. Zimmer said, "but we're wondering if . . ." He turned to Blos. "What's the name of her friend?"

"Salman Page," Blos croaked.

"Is this Salman Page's house?"

The woman shook her head.

"The boy's gone," the man at the TV said. "Better that way."

Mr. Zimmer glanced at him but addressed the woman.

"Was Lu here earlier?"

She nodded.

"Two, three hours ago."

Mr. Zimmer thought that over.

"How long did Lu stay?"

"A couple of minutes," the woman said.

"I told her to leave," the man said.

"Now, Ozzy, the man's looking for his daughter."

Ozzy shrugged and turned back to the TV.

"Do you know where she went?" Mr. Zimmer asked.

The woman blinked before answering.

"No."

Mr. Zimmer pulled his fingers through his hair.

Blos knew there were only two ways out. Through the woods or on the road. He had to ask.

"Did Lu . . . did Lu walk?"

The woman stared at Blos.

"She did. There was no car."

"Do you know which way she went?" Mr. Zimmer said.

The woman shifted.

"I heard a crash out back. It made the trailer shake. I ran to the window to see if something had landed on the chicken coop—and I saw your daughter heading back 'round the front of the trailer."

"Did you see where she went from there?"

The woman shook her head.

"The road . . . ," Blos said. He darted out of the trailer. Lu had taken the road. And if she followed Route 51, it would be miles longer to get back to her house. Miles. It was not like cutting through the woods. She was walking all the way around. Blos would run after her. He would catch up. Lu needed him. Now.

Blos had run halfway to Route 51 when the red van pulled alongside him. Mr. Zimmer rolled down the window.

"Get in, Blos. We'll be faster this way."

Blos hesitated.

"Two people are better than one," Mr. Zimmer said.

Okay, Blos thought. He climbed in.

Driving slowly, Mr. Zimmer came to the side street they had come out of on their way to the trailer. He turned on his signal light to show that he was going to turn.

That was wrong, Blos thought. Wrong.

"No!" he yelled.

Mr. Zimmer jumped.

"No, what, Blos?"

"Not that way."

Mr. Zimmer stared at him. Blos pointed down Route 51. "That way."

"But this is faster, Blos."

"Lu does not know that way."

Mr. Zimmer stared down the side street and up Route 51.

"You're right."

He turned off the turn signal and drove slowly along Route 51.

Blos stared hard. He did not see too well in the gloom. And there were cars. Lots of cars. Lots of cars not moving too fast because of the traffic and the wind and the rain and the gray.

Blos leaned forward, clutching the dashboard. They had been driving for minutes, but to Blos it felt like an hour. He craned his neck this way and that. They passed a car dealership, office buildings, a bus shelter.

"Stop!" Blos yelled.

Mr. Zimmer jolted to a stop. Blos jumped out of the van. The bus shelter! He ran back to it. There was someone in there. In the corner. Huddled.

"Lu! . . . Lu! . . . Lu! . . ."

He began shaking her. She was pale and shivering. She opened her eyes.

"Blos?"

A few seconds later, Mr. Zimmer ran up. "Omigod."

He swooped her up, as if she were a little kid, and ran back with her to the van. Blos hesitated. But only for a split second. He no longer felt queasy. He had found Lu. Now she was going home.

## 34 – Lu-Ellen Zimmer

### A good friend

Exposure had worsened whatever cold Lu had. She developed a fever that spiked and made her delirious.

"Something about a crow attacking you," Ron later told her.

"Dad almost took you to the hospital," Ricky added. "But then the Tylenol kicked in and you went back to sleep."

When Lu was finally well enough to sit up and pay attention to what was going on, Mom sat at her bedside, a bowl of soup in her hands.

"Eat some of this, dear. It'll help."

"Mom?"

"That's me."

"You're home!"

"Been here since the day before yesterday."

"But you'll catch my cold!"

Mom shook her head.

"Stupid doctors. I had to yell at them to discharge me. There are more diseases in any hospital than at home."

"But the baby . . ."

"Is fine. She's been fine all along. Don't you worry."

Lu focused on the space around her. This wasn't her bedroom.

"Where am I?"

"In the guest room, dear. We decided to keep you down here."

Lu tried to remember what had happened, how she had gotten here, but everything was too fuzzy. The last thing she remembered with some clarity was Blos Pease, shaking her awake, and then Dad . . .

"Is Blos here?" she said.

"Not at the moment," Mom said. "I expect he'll come after school. He's bicycled every day to see how you're doing."

Lu shut her eyes.

"Every . . . day?"

She reopened them. Mom nodded.

"He's the one who found you, you know."

Yes, Lu did. "He's a good guy," she said.

Mom nodded again. "Yes."

"How long have I been . . ."

"Well, today's Monday."

Lu did a quick calculation—three days. She'd been out of it for three days. And she hadn't called Salman!

She pushed aside her covers and swung her legs over—well, she tried. Somehow, they weren't doing what she was asking them to do.

"Slow down, Lu."

Mom put the bowl of soup on the side table and helped Lu turn in bed.

"You're still sick. And you're probably pretty weak."

She felt Mom's gentle hands placing slippers on her feet. Lu tried to stand. She was so unsteady!

"Hold on to me," Mom said.

Step by step, they made it to the bathroom.

"I'll manage," Lu said.

Mom smiled.

"Of course you will."

She helped Lu back to bed. Lu was exhausted by the short trip down the hall. She lay back on her pillows and shut her eyes while Mom tucked covers around her.

"Sleep," Mom said. "It'll help you heal."

Lu opened her eyes.

"Wait. Mom . . ."

"Yes?"

"Did you find a business card in my pockets?"

Mom looked puzzled.

"Dad's the one who took your clothes," she said. "He never mentioned a card."

Lu shut her eyes again. Did Dad check her jacket? she wondered. That's where it would have been. But she fell asleep before she could say the words.

She woke up to Mom's hand on her forehead.

"Lu? Can you wake up for a bit? Someone's here to see you."

Lu worked hard to shake off the grogginess. Mom helped her sit up and gave her some water to drink.

"Who . . ." She forced her eyes open. "Who's here?"

"Blos," Mom said. "I thought you'd want to see him."

Yes, Lu thought. She tried to smile.

"I'll bring him in," Mom said.

A second later, Mom returned with Blos.

"Hi, Blos," Lu said.

"Hi," Blos said.

He stood by the door, stiff and even more awkward than usual.

"I'll go check something in the kitchen," Mom said. "Why don't you sit in this chair, Blos?"

Blos sat in the chair Mom had used earlier. Lu saw worry in his eyes. His jacket, still zipped to his chin, smelled of outdoors—she breathed in the cool crispness. He laid his backpack on the floor—he must have come straight from school.

Blos sat and stared at her—a combination of fear and curiosity. Lu knew she had to speak first.

"So, how's it going?"

Blos startled. He stared down at his hands.

"O-okay."

"Mom tells me you saved my life."

He squirmed in his seat. He seemed ready to run. She didn't want him to go.

"Thank you," she said. "You're a good friend."

Blos looked up, surprise and pleasure flashing across his face. She had never seen him show so many emotions before. They were so close to the surface.

"Are you . . . are you okay?" he asked.

She smiled.

"Not quite yet," she said. "But I'm getting better."

Blos nodded.

"I . . . I have something for you."

Lu leaned forward as Blos began rummaging through his pack. He pulled out a small business card—wrinkled and slightly torn—and handed it to her. The social worker's card!

"How did you get it?" she asked.

Blos stared at her for a moment, looking confused.

"You gave it to me. In the van. You said to keep it and not to lose it. I kept it."

She gripped the card. It was her key to find Salman. As soon as she was strong enough, she'd call. Maybe she'd even get to speak to him!

"What is . . . what is the card for?" Blos asked.

Lu stared at Blos, uncertain about what to say. Blos

was Salman's friend, too. If she told Blos what the card was for, then *he'd* call. She wouldn't be first. And Salman had to know how much she cared for him.

She briefly shut her eyes.

"My mother . . . my mother said I should not ask you too many questions," Blos said. "Is that too many questions?"

He did not hide his disappointment—Lu wondered if he even knew how.

What had Salman said once? Yes. Blos was real. And Blos's friendship with her was real—that was why he was here. That was why he'd gone looking for her in the storm. That was why she was glad to see him.

"No, Blos. Not too many questions. The card has Salman's social worker's phone number."

"Does she know where he is?"

Lu nodded.

"Will you call her?" he said.

Lu extended the card.

"Why don't you?"

He stared at her hand, stricken.

"I . . . I do not . . . I do not know what to say."

"Tell her who you are. Tell her you'd like to be able to get in touch with him."

Blos still seemed uncertain. Lu felt weaker. Whatever energy she'd had was seeping away. She pulled herself together and sat forward, thrusting the card into his hand.

"Tell her, Blos. Tell her you're Salman's friend. One of the best he could ever hope for."

She wasn't sure whether he was frightened or pleased. But he sat straight in the chair, taller than ever. She sank back onto her pillows. That last outburst had exhausted her.

"You can do it, Blos. I'm counting on it."

# 35—Salman Page

**Get well soon**

Dear Lu,

My social worker, Paula Lloyd, told me that you and Blos were trying to reach me. I sent a note to the school for you, the day after I left—but Paula says I didn't have the right address. My new address is at the bottom of this note. The group home is pretty good about mail, and close to Springfalls. They also have a computer we're allowed to use. The house supervisor told me he can create an e-mail address for me, so send me yours.

Tina Royal also called Paula and told her what had happened. Tina said that she had spoken to your parents, and they said you're getting better.

I'm sorry, Lu. I'm sorry I left without saying goodbye. I'm sorry that you came looking for me, and I wasn't there. I'm sorry my first note never got to you. But when Paula told me Blos had called—I was so happy. I do want to stay in touch.

Get well soon, Lu. Write when you are able. I promise to write back.

Salman

P.S. Look out for Bird. He likes shiny things.

# 36

## D.B.'S AT SPRINGFALLS JUNIOR HIGH

**by Lu-Ellen Zimmer**
**photo by Blos Pease**

This fall I became a designated buddy. I had had a d.b. in seventh grade. I thought I knew everything there was to know: a d.b. shows new students around the school; a d.b. teaches new kids the rules. I didn't know a d.b. could really be a friend.

"The d.b. program is what distinguishes Spring-falls from the other junior high schools in the area," Vice Principal Frank Phillip claims. Springfalls

Junior High is the only school in Farmington County where older students are paired up with new students to help them through the changes they face moving from elementary school to junior high.

"We're a model for the state," Superintendent Eleanor Theseus says.

Other towns, notably Watersquare, have approached Springfalls to duplicate its program.

"What counts, though, is the quality of the students mentoring," Ms. Angela Rabinowitz, adviser for the d.b. program, says.

When I was a new student last year, my d.b. walked me around, ate lunches with me, and told me how to complete assignments. She made me feel important and gave the school a friendly face. And so when I became a d.b., I did the same. I showed my assigned student how to outline a science lab report. I sat with him in the cafeteria at lunch. And I took him around the school grounds.

I didn't expect to learn from him, too.

"Every student is different," Ms. Rabinowitz explains. "A d.b. can help a new student get through the confusion of the first few days of school. In return, the d.b. meets a new and interesting person. And, with luck, both students grow."

Salman Page, my assigned student, taught me things. He demonstrated how to can vegetables.

He showed me how to approach a wild crow without frightening it. He also taught me that finding a genuine friend is tricky, but worth it in the end.

"We hope each new student and designated buddy pairing works," Ms. Rabinowitz says. "At the very least we expect each new student to start the school year with more confidence than he or she might have without a d.b."

And sometimes it is the d.b. who gains confidence from the new student.

# 37 – Puck

### A boon

Fate had been kind. Our king and queen reconciled. And I was dismissed! I had not expected this turn of events.

When I had delivered the queen's message, the king paled.

"Where did you get this circlet?"

I opted for the simplest answer.

"The queen gave it to me to give to you."

He stared at it for a second. I feared my part in all of this, but his next question saved me.

"How was the circlet found?"

I would have smiled if I could!

"A crow retrieved it on Nimue's island."

He buried his head in his hands. Some truths are

more powerful than others. When he looked up, he almost appeared haggard.

"Where is the queen, Puck? I need to find her."

And so I led him to her. She remained impassive at his approach, but I could see the hint of pleasure in her eyes. I was told to wait, at a distance, and could not make out their words. But the king bent to his knees, and the queen's shoulders softened. I waited for a long time, hoping the king had not forgotten that he had instructed me to stay.

I was nodding, almost asleep, when I was summoned anew. The king and queen held hands. The circlet lay on the king's wrist.

"It is a new day, Puck," the queen announced, "and we start afresh."

I bowed with naught to say.

"You have served me faithfully." She glanced at the king. "Both of us faithfully. And if I recall, you have lost a pie tin in the bargain."

The king's smile was mischievous. I dared not look him in the eye.

"So I shall grant you a boon."

"A boon, milady?"

The queen smiled at that. "A boon worth the value of a pie tin."

It should have been a boon worth the value of the circlet, but I did not protest. The king and queen were in a generous mood. It wasn't my place to try them.

"I ask to be relieved from spying on the boy."

King Oberon laughed. "You cannot ask for that."

I looked at him, dismayed.

"You have already been relieved," he continued. "We *both* have decided that the boy is now a man. The queen has fulfilled the promise to his mother. And he is no longer of any interest to Faery."

I could ask for something else! A boon. Anything I desired. I thought for a moment.

"I request . . . ," I hesitated. But the king's amusement made me bold. "I request peace between Faery and the crow."

The queen raised an eyebrow.

"Peace?"

Oberon's puzzled face emboldened me further.

"As an honored ally."

The queen considered this. An alliance was a kind of friendship that carried liabilities of its own—as well she knew. But she had offered me a boon. Anything I desired. She knew that, too. And she *was* in a generous mood.

"To this crow, Puck, it shall be granted. Though I wonder at the wisdom of this bargain."

She paused, letting her smile tell me that for today she would indulge me, even if she thought this a flawed boon. "You are dismissed."

And so I was bound for the pleasures of mischief. Without the king and queen.

# 38 – Salman Page

### Good news

Salman sat in the classroom, making sure his face betrayed none of his nervousness. His adviser had signed him up for the Creative Writing Club.

"Your Language Arts teacher at your old school recommended you," the man said. "It'll be a good way to meet people."

Salman hadn't been given a choice.

Kids were trickling in, saying hello to each other. A few gave Salman a nod—friendly, Salman thought. They sat on desks around the room. The leader, a boy named Colin, perched himself in front.

"Welcome, all. I am pleased to announce that we have a new member—Salman Page."

Salman waved. A smattering of *hi*'s and *welcome*'s greeted him.

"We usually begin each meeting by sharing one item of good news. Want to start us off, Tanika?"

A small girl with her hair in braids stood.

"My sister didn't snore last night."

Giggles.

"I found my missing key," a boy said.

"The Celtics won yesterday," a girl said.

One after another, kids sat or stood and shared small snippets of news. Some were silly. Some were funny. Some were nice.

"What about you, Salman?" Colin said.

Salman thought for a moment.

"I got a letter from a friend."

"Sweet!" Tanika said.

Lu had sent him news of her recovery. And Blos had sent him a photo of a frog.

"Now that we've shared news, who has something to read for us?" Colin asked.

Salman sat back. Another girl stepped forward, poem in hand. This might not be so bad. And as kids began offering advice on how to improve her work, he began composing a new letter to Lu and Blos in his head.

"Dear Lu and Blos," it'd begin. "There's a bus that goes to Springfalls. . . ."

# 39 – Lu-Ellen Zimmer

**Beauty and grace**

Lu waved to Ruthie after band.

"Call me tonight," Ruthie said.

Lu grinned.

"Will do."

But first, she had an appointment to keep. Blos waited for her at the bleachers. They climbed about one-third of the way up. Not at the top, where kids might think they were out to prove something. Nor at the bottom, where kids might think they were timid. But in the middle, where they weren't obvious.

Lu checked the fields, the metal whistle cupped in her hands.

A murder of crows wheeled around tall trees at the edge of the baseball field.

She blew the whistle once and then allowed the sun to flicker off its shiny surface. When one of the birds, larger than the rest, broke off from the murder, she pocketed the toy.

"Keep the bottle cap in the sunshine," she said.

Blos grinned.

Bird was flying to them.

# Acknowledgments

I fell in love with William Shakespeare's *A Midsummer Night's Dream* when I was a teenager and saw a magical production of the play in Montreal. Watching fairies frolic in gossamer costumes, while the king and queen of the fairies schemed and the humans played buffoons, enchanted me. Over the years I have seen many more productions of the play, read a children's version by John Updike, and studied the play's text.

Despite my continued love for the play, something bothered me. The reason for Queen Titania and King Oberon's dispute was jealousy over a changeling, a young boy referred to as a page. But the child spoke no lines. He did not show up in any of the stage directions. And in the productions I have seen, he never appeared onstage. So I wondered, what happened to this boy? A few years ago, I began writing about Salman Page.

I have received a lot of help since that first inspiration. I want to thank: the Eppler-Epsteins, who reassured me that this was a story worth telling; Sanna Stanley, Meg Greene, Paula Feder, and Nada Fuleihan, who gave generous input in early drafts; Lisa Findlay, who convinced me that magic was key to making the story come to life; Jane Brown, who took time to review the manuscript and give me valuable insights about Asperger's; the Shoreline Society of Children's Book Writers and Illustrators, whose members over the years have provided feedback and encouragement; and all of my friends and family, who have continued to support me in so many ways.

Special thanks go to my agent, Rachel Orr, for her strong faith in the value of the text. And I give an extra thank-you to my editor, R. Schuyler Hooke, who struggled harder than anyone else to help me make the story come out just right.

Last but never least, I thank my children, who put up with a distracted mother when I worked on the manuscript, and my husband, Jon, who, in addition to convincing me it was all possible, helped me solve thorny plot points by lending an endlessly patient ear.

A. C. E. Bauer has been telling and writing stories since childhood. Her first middle-grade novel, *No Castles Here*, was chosen for the American Library Association Rainbow List and was named "one of the strongest titles of the year" in a starred notice in *Kirkus Reviews*. Born and raised in Montreal, she spends most of the year in New England, and much of the summer on a lake in Quebec. To learn more about A. C. E. Bauer and her writing, visit her Web site at www.acebauer.com.